Geronimo Stilton

Thea Stilton

THE TREASURE SEEKERS

Scholastic Inc.

Published by Scholastic Inc., *Publishers since 1920*, 557 Broadway, New York, NY 10012. SCHOLASTIC and associated logos are trademarks and/or registered trademarks of Scholastic Inc.

Library of Congress Cataloging-in-Publication Data available

ISBN 978-1-338-30617-0

Text by Thea Stilton
Original title *Alla ricerca dei tesori perduti*
Cover by Giuseppe Facciotto and Flavio Ferron
Illustrations by Giuseppe Facciotto, Chiara Balleello, Barbara Pellizzari, Valeria Brambilla, and Alessandro Muscillo
Graphics by Chiara Cebraro

Special thanks to AnnMarie Anderson
Translated by Julia Heim
Interior design by Becky James

10 9 8 7 6 5 4 3 2 1 19 20 21 22 23

Printed in China 62

First edition, March 2019

Dear friends,

We've just returned from an adventure we will never forget! It started as a simple vacation in Scotland, but it took us far away as we followed the tracks of a very special mouse who lived many, many years ago. Slowly we brought to light her great secret, which was tied to some of the most precious treasures our planet has to offer. In the process, we found ourselves traveling the world, visiting enchanted places, meeting marvemouse friends, and uncovering intriguing mysteries.

You can find out about the rest of our adventure by reading these pages. We hope the trip will be as exciting to you as it was to us!

Big hugs from the Thea Sisters,

PAULINA

Violet

Colette

AIRLINES

FLIGHT: R 375

FROM: Mouseford Academy, Whale Island

TO: Edinburgh, Scotland

N° 036428

MEET THE THEA SISTERS!

Colette

She has a real passion for clothing and accessories, especially pink ones. When she is older she wants to be a fashion writer.

Paulina

She is generous and cheerful, and she loves traveling and meeting new people all over the world. She has a real knack for science and technology.

Violet

She loves reading and learning about new things. She likes classical music and dreams of becoming a famouse violinist!

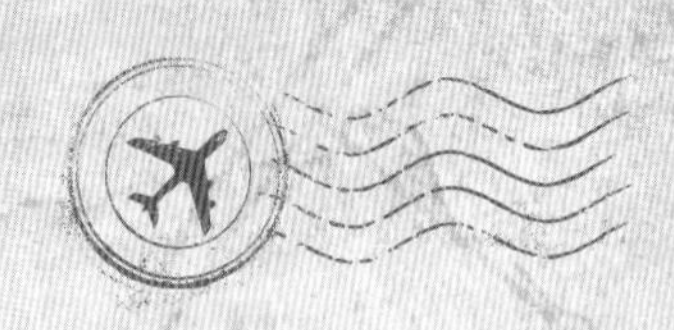

Nicky

She comes from Australia and is passionate about sports, ecology, and nature. She loves the open air and is always on the move!

Pamela

She is a skilled mechanic: Give her a screwdriver and she can fix anything! She loves to cook. Her favorite food is pizza, and she would eat it every moment of every day if she could.

Do you want to be a Thea Sister?

....

I like . . . ____________

____

____

____

____

____

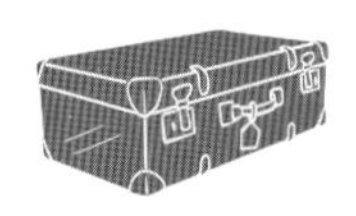

A SCOTTISH DREAM COME TRUE

Colette placed the last clip in her fur and smiled in satisfaction.

"There!" she squeaked. "I'm ready!"

She went to join the Thea Sisters in the room they had been sharing for a few weeks. But instead of finding her four best friends, she found only one.

"Where are the others?" Colette asked Violet, who was happily stuffing a backpack with a blanket, a travel pillow, and a camera.

"Nicky is feeding the horses before we go," Violet explained. "Pam is in the kitchen making sandwiches, and Paulina —"

Before Violet could finish her sentence, the door flew open and Paulina entered, a **MAP** in her paws.

"For our picnic, Miss Kerr suggested we take the trail into the woods a few miles from here," she announced, excitedly pointing to a spot on the **MAP**. "She says there's a peaceful clearing with a lovely stream running through it."

"That sounds so beautiful!" Colette said, sighing wistfully. She LOOKED out the window at the bright emerald-green grass and the sheep, cows, and ponies that Nicky was feeding for the last time. "Oh, I'm so sad to be leaving Scotland already. This vacation went by too quickly!"

Ready to go?
I'm ready!

"You're right, Coco," Paulina agreed, "but it's not over yet!"

"Exactly," Violet added. "Let's enjoy the days we have left."

The friends smiled as they reflected on the wonderful vacation. It wasn't very long ago that Colette, Paulina, Violet, Nicky, and Pamela were at Mouseford Academy thinking about how they would spend their summer, when Paulina found an ad that seemed perfect for them.

> **Do you want a different kind of vacation?**
>
> **Scotland is waiting!**
>
> Stay at an organic farm for free! In exchange, you'll help us take care of the garden and animals.

The Thea Sisters were excited by the idea

of visiting a beautiful farm where they would learn to take care of sheep and horses.

They immediately got in touch with Miss Kerr, the owner of the farm. Then they booked their flight from Whale Island and, in a short time, found themselves driving through the green countryside on their

SCOTLAND

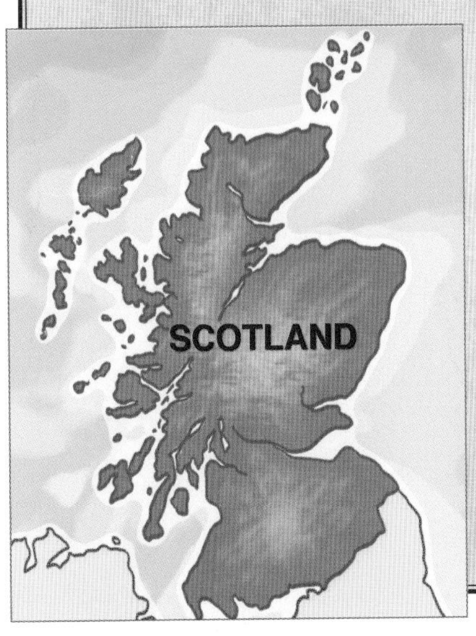

Scotland is one of the four regions that make up the United Kingdom, along with Wales, England, and Northern Ireland. It covers the northern third of the island of Great Britain, and its landscape is rich with striking mountains, blue lakes, thick forests, and golden beaches. The famouse Scottish Highlands region is known for its wild nature and beautiful castles.

way to Miss Kerr's farm. That's how their very special summer started!

Yum . . . shortbread!

When the Thea Sisters arrived at the farm, Miss Kerr greeted them warmly and made them feel right at home with some of her delicious shortbreads — Scottish **butter cookies** — and *cranachan*, a ***traditional*** dessert made with raspberries, oats, honey, and cream.

Seals on the Scottish coast.

Taking care of the garden and the animals was, of course, work, but it was also fun. Nicky in particular had really taken to two of the ponies on the farm. Plus, the five friends had rented an SUV and visited the surrounding areas, where they explored breathtaking WATERFALLS, CAVES, bays, and castles.

A charming Scottish castle.

The vacation had gone by in a flash, and they were almost at the end. Miss Kerr had suggested that the mouselets rest and visit all the things they hadn't seen before they had to leave. So that day the Thea Sisters had organized a relaxing picnic, and now they couldn't wait for their adventure.

"We have enough sandwiches for a week!" Pam exclaimed as she returned from

the kitchen holding a basket of food, napkins, and utensils.

"And I've loaded the backpacks with everything we need," Violet said.

"Great!" Colette exclaimed. "Now let's get Nicky and go!"

A SUDDEN STORM

Half an hour later, Pam parked the SUV in a small parking lot at the edge of the woods.

"Here we are!" Paulina exclaimed happily. "The place Miss Kerr suggested is about a ten-minute HIKE down this trail."

Pam looked at the trailhead, confused. "It looks like three different paths begin here," she pointed out. "Did Miss Kerr mention which trail to take?"

Paulina scratched her head. "I don't know," she said, perplexed. "On the map, there's only one. Maybe they all lead to the same place."

"Maybe, or maybe not," Colette said wisely. "We'd better check!"

At that moment, a hiker approached and Colette flagged the mouse down.

"Excuse me," Colette asked, politely pointing to the map. "But could you tell me what path we should take to get **HERE**?"

The hiker barely glanced at the map. Instead she just looked up at the sky and shook her head. "**It's not worth it,**" she said.

Colette was surprised. According to Miss Kerr, the spot sounded like the perfect place.

"But why not?" Colette replied. "We heard it was a nice spot for a PICNIC."

"Suit yourself," the rodent replied brusquely. "Take the first path on the left."

Colette went back to her friends to tell them the mouse's **answer**.

"How strange," Violet said.

"Maybe she just meant that there are **better** places around here," Nicky said with a shrug.

"There's only one way to find out," Pamela said **confidently**, and the five friends started down the trail. A short while later, they emerged from the woods in a beautiful clearing with a **spectacular** view of the mountains.

"Well, this place seems absolutely **perfect** to me!" Colette exclaimed happily. "There are so many flowers! And look at this **sparkling**, clear stream. I don't know what that mouse was talking about!"

How beautiful!
Let's set up here!

What lovely butterflies.

"Yes, but be careful not to fall in," Pam warned. "The water will be cold."

Paulina laid the blankets on the grass and the FIVE FRIENDS could finally relax and enjoy the marvemouse view.

"Come on, let's take a photo!" Colette proposed as she finished the last bite of a piece of the cake that Miss Kerr had packed them.

"Oh, I think we've taken enough photos on this trip," Violet said as she lay back on the blanket and closed her eyes. "Right now, I just want to relax."

But a moment later, Violet sat straight up on the blanket.

"Hey!" she squeaked. "Who splashed me with water?"

Nicky looked worriedly at the sky, which had suddenly gone DARK.

"It wasn't us, Vi," she explained, pointing to the gray clouds thickening above them. "It looks like it's about to **STORM**!"

She had barely finished her sentence when there was a **CLAP** of thunder and thick sheets of rain began to fall.

"**LET'S GO!**" Paulina yelled, quickly stuffing the blankets in the backpacks. She left one blanket out so she and her friends could shelter themselves from the rain.

"Hurry!" Nicky said. "Let's get back to the car."

But suddenly she stopped. A single hiker had been walking near the stream, and Nicky saw him slip on the **ROCKS**.

"I'll be right back!" she called to her friends. Then she pulled her hood over her head and **scampered** to the shore. There, a blond mouse was sitting on the ground

holding his paw.

"What happened?" Nicky asked.

"I hurt my ankle!" he replied, his snout twisting in **pain**.

"Come on, lean on me!" Nicky said as she helped him up.

"**OUCH!**" he squeaked. "I don't think I can walk!"

"But we have to get out of this storm," Nicky insisted.

Suddenly, Nicky remembered seeing a small stone building near the shore, not too far away. It was definitely CLOSER than the car! She motioned to the Thea Sisters to follow her there.

A few minutes later, their fur **SOAKED**, Nicky and the hiker managed to make their way to the building's covered porch.

"**THANKS!**" the ratlet said to Nicky. "Without your help, I never would have managed. My name is Boyd, and I live **nearby**. I went out for a walk, and when the storm came, I tried to hurry, but I slipped on the **ROCKS**!"

A soft voice behind them interrupted: **"YOU'VE ALL BEEN THOUGHTLESS!"**

UNEXPECTED HELP

Colette turned toward the door: She had heard that voice before! It was the mouse she had asked for directions!

The mouse looked at them sternly and repeated herself. "**YOU'VE ALL BEEN THOUGHTLESS!** It was clear a big storm was coming."

Then she turned to Colette. "I tried to warn you . . ."

"I'm sorry I didn't understand you," Colette said apologetically. "But we're not used to the weather here, so we didn't see the **signs** of the storm."

"Achoo!" Nicky sneezed suddenly.

"It's my fault," Boyd chimed in. "They stayed back to help me."

The mouse noticed that Boyd was balancing on one paw to keep the **injured** one off the ground. Then, without another squeak, she gestured for all of them to come inside.

"You'll catch a cold out here, especially you two," she said to Nicky and Boyd.

The group ENTERED the house, which was incredibly warm and dry thanks to the FIRE burning in a large stone fireplace.

Their host headed to a corner of the big room, which was furnished with rustic WOOD furniture. Then she took a blanket out of a chest and gave it to Nicky before leading Boyd to a chair to examine his ankle.

Nicky wrapped herself in the blanket as her friends stood next to her. Paulina began to pet the cute dog that was curled up on the thick carpet.

"Your ankle is **swelling** up quite a

bit," their host said. "A doctor should take a look at it."

"I should go home so my **PARENTS** can take me to the hospital," Boyd said. "I don't live far from here, but I don't know how I'll get there!"

"That's **no problem**," Pam exclaimed. "My friends and I will go get our car, and we'll **TAKE YOU** home right away!"

"But we won't all fit," Paulina pointed out. "If you take Boyd, one of us will have to stay here . . ."

Their host decided for them.

"**She stays here**," she declared, pointing to a **shivering** Nicky, who was still wrapped in a blanket. "I'll get her some dry clothes and a cup of hot tea."

"And I'll stay here with her!" Colette said.

So Pam, Paulina, and Violet hurried to get the **SUV** so they could take Boyd home.

Meanwhile, Nicky put on the **dry clothes** the woman had brought her: wide short pants, a pair of knee-length socks, and an argyle sweater.

"I **wore** those when I was your age!" the

older mouse said, smiling. "They're a little outdated, but they suit you **perfectly**!"

"Oh, they're perfect, Miss . . ."

"Beitris," she said, introducing herself. Then she pointed to a bench in front of the crackling FIREPLACE and added: "Have a seat and I'll make you some tea."

Then she disappeared into the kitchen.

"Coco, what do you think of my look?" Nicky joked, spinning around and posing like she was about to have her picture taken. "Colette?"

Her friend hadn't heard her because she was busy admiring the biggest decoration in the room:

How do I look?

a tapestry hanging over the fireplace. The embroidery featured a huge, lush tree with deep ROOTS surrounded by a frame of leaves and flowers.

"This is such a beautiful design!" Nicky exclaimed.

"Yes, it's really lovely!" Colette said in admiration. "The leaves, trunk, and flowers are stitched in such detail."

"And the design is so BaLanCeD," Nicky said as she leaned close to the tapestry to get a better LOOK.

At that moment, Beitris entered the room holding a tray with a teapot and teacups.

"**WHAT ARE YOU DOING?**" she asked brusquely.

In the land where sweet winds blow. Follow the petals: What lies below? Remember:
Midnight comes along before the sun rises amid birdsong. There you will find a priceless delight: An alabaster
garden, true and bright. Created by one who was dear and true to the jewel of
the palace, like me to you. The guard is a friend with feet so deep. In its arms this precious gift will keep.
ALABASTER GARDEN

THE LEGEND OF THE TAPESTRY

Nicky stepped away from the tapestry.

"We were just admiring this beautiful piece," Colette replied tentatively.

Beitris was quiet for a long moment. Then she sighed.

"I'm sorry, I didn't mean to be RUDE," she said. "I'm afraid I'm not used to having guests. As you may have guessed, that isn't a simple tapestry . . ."

At that moment, Pam, Paulina, and Violet knocked on the door and entered. They had returned after taking Boyd home.

"Make yourselves comfortable," Beitris said.

"Thank you, but we don't want to disturb

you too much," Violet replied politely.

Beitris shook her head. "You're not disturbing me," she said. "And it's better if you wait here for a bit. The storm will stop soon."

"But how do you know that?" Pam asked, surprised.

The older mouse smiled.

"Oh, I've always lived in this valley," she explained. "I know every sign of nature in this corner of the world. I just have to LOOK at the color of the sky and the shape of the clouds, or smell the scent of the woods to know if it will rain or if it will be a cold winter. Nature talks to us, and I've been able to understand since I was a little mouselet. I use my senses: I look, I listen, I feel, and I smell!"

Colette nodded and looked more carefully

Make yourselves comfortable!

What a lovely fireplace!

around the room. She could see that it was full of signs of nature: vases of plants and GREENERY, pinecones decorating the stone fireplace, and of course the tapestry she had admired earlier.

As she sat next to Nicky in front of the fireplace, happily sipping a cup of tea, Colette gathered her courage and asked Beitris the question that was on her mind.

"Can you tell us more about this fascinating tapestry?" she asked.

Beitris nodded. She sat in a rocking chair, petting her dog, who sat curled at her feet.

"The tapestry belonged to my great-aunt," Beitris began.

"So it's a family HEIRLOOM," Nicky remarked.

"Oh, it's much more than that," Beitris replied. "That tapestry hides a true mystery."

"A **MYSTERY**?" Pam asked, intrigued. "What kind of mystery?"

"Well, you noticed the writing around the edges, right?" Beitris noted. "It's a **SECRET MESSAGE** that my great-aunt left to my grandmother Petra many years ago. No one has ever managed to **DECIPHER** its true meaning!"

A clap of thunder rang out suddenly, and the five friends jumped.

"It's a message that speaks of petals, of midnight, and of a mysterious, hidden ALABASTER GARDEN," Beitris continued. "Supposedly a precious, ancient treasure is buried there."

"So it's like a fable?" Paulina asked. "It's a LEGEND invented to intrigue the listener."

"Yes, that's what everyone thinks," Beitris replied, slowly sipping her tea. "Well, almost everyone."

At that moment, a ray of sunshine came through the window. The dark clouds in the sky had disappeared, and the rain had stopped, leaving behind sparkling beads of water that glistened like jewels on the pinecones.

Before the mouselets could say anything

more, Beitris stood up.

"It's best if you go **RIGHT NOW**," she said abruptly. "It will start raining again soon."

The Thea Sisters were a bit **SURPRISED**, but they nodded and quickly stood up.

"Thank you again," Nicky said as they bid Beitris farewell. "We will be back **TOMORROW** to return your clothes."

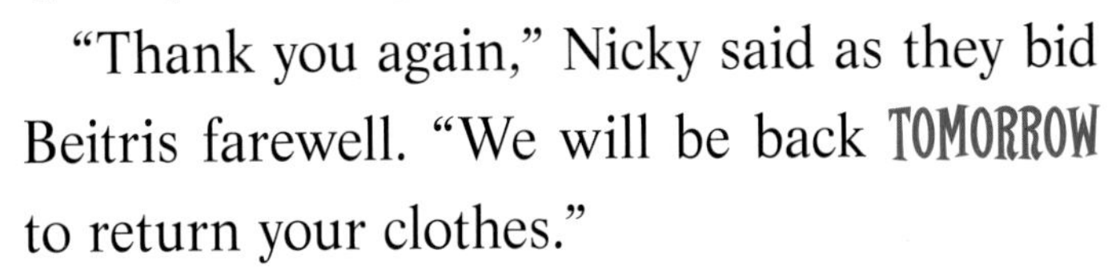

The five friends were quiet during their trip back to the farm. When they were about halfway there, the skies opened up and a light rain began to fall, just as Beitris had predicted.

AN UNFRIENDLY VISIT

The next day, the mouselets woke up early. They wanted to help Miss Kerr pick the vegetables in the garden one last time before they returned the clothes to Beitris.

A few hours later, when Pam parked the SUV in front of Beitris's house, the friends knew at once that something strange was going on. The door to the house was wide open and another SUV was parked nearby. The Thea Sisters exchanged GLANCES and silently approached the kitchen window.

The room was empty, but a few of the chairs had been **knocked over** and a vase full of wild flowers that had been on the table lay **smashed** on the floor.

"Oh no!" Paulina gasped. "Something must have happened!"

"Let's LOOK in the living room," Violet whispered, pointing to a window nearby.

When they ***peered*** into the living room, the Thea Sisters were shocked at what they saw. Beitris was on her feet in the middle of the room, trying to fend off two intruders.

A fourth mouse stood in a dark corner, her snout hidden by a pair of large **sunglasses** and a black hat. She was giving the intruders orders. The intruders grabbed Beitris suddenly, pinning her arms behind her back.

There was **NO TIME** to lose: The Thea Sisters had to do something **RIGHT AWAY**!

"Pam, run to the SUV and start honking the horn!" Violet ordered. "Let's try to scare them off. We'll GO INSIDE and free Beitris!"

Pam ran to the SUV while Violet, Nicky, Paulina, and Colette **BURST** into the house, squeaking **LOUDLY**.

"GET YOUR PAWS OFF HER!" Colette cried. "**LEAVE HER BE!**"

The three intruders looked at one another, stunned.

"Where did they come from?" one of the big, burly mice asked.

Stop her!
What do you want?

The mysterious mouse in the black hat scowled.

"I don't know, but these four won't ruin our plans!" she snarled. Then she turned to one of the big mice. "Take care of them!"

But at that moment, Pam started to honk the horn.

BEEP! BEEP! BEEP!

The three intruders jumped. Colette took advantage of their surprise.

"Here comes our BACKUP," she shouted loudly. "WE'RE NOT ALONE!"

The mouse in the hat made an angry gesture and turned to her accomplices.

"YOU take the tapestry!" she barked at one of them. "Let's get out of here, quick!"

Before the Thea Sisters could come up with a plan, the first mouse grabbed the tapestry from the wall and the second one let go of Beitris. As soon as her paws were free, Beitris elbowed him in the side.

"Ouch!" he complained.

"Stop whining and run!" his sidekick said, dragging him out of the house.

The three quickly reached their SUV and **zoomed** away, disappearing from the Thea Sisters' sight as they looked on from the doorway. Then Colette, Violet, Paulina, and Nicky gathered around Beitris. Paulina leaned down to pet and comfort the dog, who was still barking.

"Are you okay?" Colette asked Beitris, worried.

"**I'm okay**," the elderly mouse squeaked softly. "But it's only because of you five. I don't know how to thank you."

"I called the police!" Pam said, rushing back into the house from the Thea Sisters'

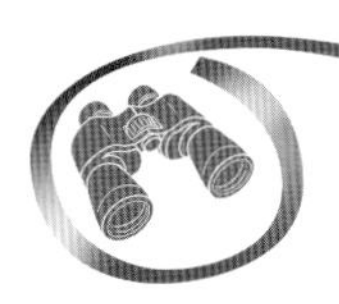

SUV. "They'll be here shortly. Did they take anything?"

"My tapestry," Beitris replied, sighing heavily. "And I think I know why. Sit down and I'll tell you everything. I know now that I can **trust** you."

THE STORY OF A. B. LANE

Beitris sat down in the rocking chair, and the Thea Sisters sat down around her, eager to find out more about the tapestry.

"Yesterday I told you that the tapestry speaks of a treasure," Beitris began, "and you believed it was a LEGEND."

Nicky and the others all nodded.

"Well, it isn't just a legend," Beitris continued. "The tapestry is really a map. It leads to treasure buried in the mysterious ALABASTER GARDEN that a mouse named Aurora Beatrix Lane discovered during her travels around the world."

"Who is Aurora Beatrix Lane?" Pamela asked.

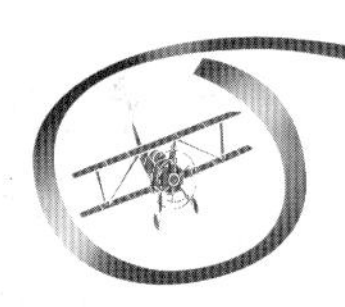

"Sorry, I'm getting ahead of myself," Beatris said. "Let me start at the **beginning** . . ."

She stood up and opened a drawer, pulling out an envelope of old, faded **pictures**. She handed one to Pamela.

"*This* is *Aurora Beatrix Lane*!" Beitris said.

The photo showed a young mouse standing next to a **biplane**. She had short, curly hair that stuck out from under a pilot's helmet, and she was smiling **BRIGHTLY**. She wore a coat over a light-colored shirt, some knee pants, a pair of high boots, and a long scarf that **fluttered** around her neck.

Nicky **EXAMINED** the photograph closely and then looked up at Beitris.

"She looks like you!" she exclaimed.

Beitris smiled. "She was one of my

grandmother Petra's six sisters," she *explained*. "I'm named after her: **Beitris** is the Scottish version of *Beatrix*.

Aurora Beatrix Lane and her biplane

"My grandmother wanted me to be named in honor of her beloved **missing** sister."

"Missing?" Colette asked, but her remark was drowned out by her friends' chatter.

"So she was a **pilot**?" Nicky asked, looking at the photo.

"Yes, she was a pilot, a motorcyclist, and an archaeologist," Beitris said with a nod. "But most of all, Aurora Beatrix Lane was a **FEARLESS EXPLORER**! My grandmother

said when Aurora was born, the Lane family became decidedly more animated. Aurora was curious and **fearless**.

"She never missed an opportunity to ***run*** and play with other children. And even as a little mouselet, she would spend hours in her room looking at maps and ATLASES. Unfortunately, this disappointed her mother — my great-grandmother — who would have preferred that she be at home embroidering

Sewing wasn't for her . . .

like the other mouselets her age."

Beitris stopped squeaking for a moment and smiled to herself as she remembered her grandmother's stories. Then she sighed and continued.

"But Aurora wasn't like the others: Lace and fancy clothes didn't interest her! She was courageous and she had a great love of adventure and MYSTERY. So she convinced her mother to send her to England for college. There she could study her real passion, archaeology.

"It wasn't

Aurora at college

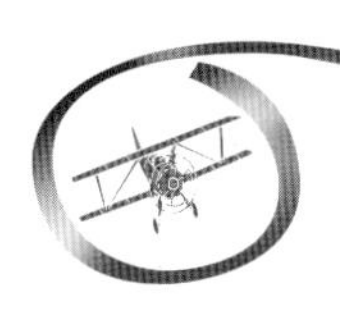

unusual for her to arrive at school wearing pants — and riding a **MOTORCYCLE**! Have a **LOOK**!"

Colette looked closely at the photo Beitris showed them.

"That must have been **SHOCKING** to some at that time," she said.

"Yes!" Beitris agreed. "Some mice certainly found Aurora **unconventional**. But she didn't mind. She was **true** to herself. And

Motorcycles: another one of her passions!

when a flight school opened near her house, she couldn't miss the **opportunity**.

"She signed up right away. Unfortunately, when the owners saw that she was female, they didn't take her **seriously**. So she jumped on her motorcycle and drove off, navigating around potholes and rocks and dodging trees and puddles. Then she drove back and gave the owners a direct order:

'Now I want you to teach me to fly as well as I can drive a motorcycle!'

A mouse quickly stepped forward and offered to be her flight instructor. His name was **Robert**. He was a young medic with a

Aurora and Robert: a special friendship!

passion for flying and delivering medicine all over the world.

"They grew close immediately, even if they were often apart while one of them was traveling. They sent each other long letters and tried to see each other as often as they could, no matter where in the WORLD they happened to be."

"What an adventurous and romantic life!" Colette exclaimed, sighing.

"Unfortunately Aurora's life took a tragic turn," Beitris continued sadly.

The mouselets GLANCED at one another in surprise as Beitris stood up and went to look out the window. Her shoulders slumped sadly. After a few moments, she turned to the five young mouselets and smiled once more.

"You've been very patient listening to my

tale," she continued. "Now I'll tell you the rest of the story and the meaning behind the **tapestry** . . ."

WHERE SWEET WINDS BLOW

Beitris sat back in her chair and continued the story, showing a new photograph:

"After getting her diploma and her pilot's license, Aurora collaborated with **Jan von Klawitz**, her archaeology professor. Klawitz considered her one of his best students, and a young talent in her field, so he often involved her in his excavations. Aurora was very passionate about that part of her life, and traveled the WORLD,

helping the professor with his numerous discoveries."

"How exciting!" Paulina commented. "Who knows how many magnificent relics she unearthed."

"Many, I'm sure," Beitris replied with a sigh. "We just have no idea **which ones** they were! Aurora kept all her destinations a **SECRET**. She only went home once after her first trip."

"Do you mean she never saw her **family** again?" Colette asked, stunned.

"Not exactly," Beitris explained. "You see, her sisters **GREW UP** and moved: My grandmother Petra married a Scottish man and came to live here in the Highlands, and the others settled in various parts of Europe and even South America. Aurora **met up** with them during her travels around the

world, but I believe she intended to return home to stay only once she had finished her archaeological adventures."

"But that's not what happened, is it?" Violet asked softly.

"It isn't," Beitris replied sadly, shaking her head. "After years of exploration, Aurora disappeared aboard her biplane under mysterious circumstances."

"Oh no!" Paulina squeaked. "But what happened to her?"

"No one knows," Beitris replied. "Since Aurora never made her destination or her travel plans public, it was impossible to piece together her last location."

"But that's terrible!" Colette cried out.

Beitris nodded. "After the first of her trips, Aurora visited my grandmother and gave her a package. She asked her to

protect it at all costs and told her never to show it to anyone."

"Was it the tapestry?" Violet guessed.

"Exactly," Beitris confirmed. "Aurora said it was a map capable of leading to a very precious treasure, but that it had to be kept a secret for a while.

"She warned my grandmother that someone **DANGEROUS** could get his or her paws on it. She asked my grandmother to take care of it and to wait for her to return.

Only then would Aurora use the map to bring to light the precious discovery she had made so she could share it with the world."

"Do you remember what was written on the tapestry?" Nicky asked Beitris.

"Of course!" Beitris replied. "I memorized it when I was five, before I learned to read. That's when my grandmother first told me Aurora's story."

Beitris closed her eyes and began to recite:

"In the land where sweet winds blow,
Follow the petals: What lies below?
Remember: Midnight comes along
before the sun rises amid birdsong.
There you will find a priceless delight,
An alabaster garden, true and bright.
Created by one who was dear and true
to the jewel of the palace, like me to you.
The guard is a friend with feet so deep,
In its arms this precious gift will keep."

"Sweet winds, **petals**, Dawn . . . This seems like a poem more than a treasure map!" Pam exclaimed.

"Or maybe it's a riddle!" Nicky added. "I can't figure out whether the jewel of the palace is the

priceless delight or the ALABASTER GARDEN . . ."

Beitris smiled.

"I know," she agreed sympathetically. "I haven't been able to figure it out, either. No one has. In the end, even my grandmother began to doubt the alabaster garden's EXISTENCE."

"And what do you think?" Violet asked.

"Oh, I think the treasure exists," Beitris said. "And those mice who stole the tapestry today prove it. But the tapestry and the poem are true puzzles."

Violet was quiet for a moment.

"Did those three mice take **anything else**?" Violet asked thoughtfully.

Beitris shook her head. "No," she replied.

"Then you're right," Violet concluded. "The robbers came here with clear intentions: They wanted to steal the **tapestry**! But who else could have known Aurora's story?"

The five friends looked at Beitris and at one another, **baffled**.

"I don't know," Beitris admitted. "Now you five should go. I've taken up too much of your **time** already. There's nothing more you can do, and the **POLICE** will be here shortly."

So the Thea Sisters said good-bye to Beitris with warm hugs. Then they returned to the farm. But they couldn't stop thinking about *Aurora's story* and the **mysterious treasure**.

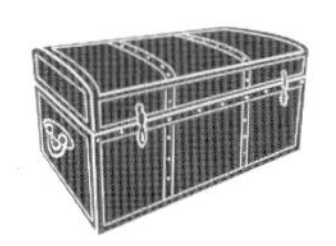

FIVE FRIENDS, ONE IDEA

The next day was the last of the Thea Sisters' vacation in Scotland. Their trip had been amazing, but they were sad, and it wasn't just because they were reluctant to leave Miss Kerr and her wonderful farm.

While they were having breakfast, Violet let out a BIG yawn.

"You know, last night I dreamed I was flying around the world on a biplane," she said. "It was exhilarating!"

Colette smiled. "I dreamed I was traveling by motorcycle while wearing a stylish red helmet!"

"And in my dreams, I was EXPLORING a South American forest where I found an incredible treasure," Pam added as she sipped her cup of tea. "It was an enormouse chest full of nothing but **chocolate**!"

The friends giggled at Pam's tale.

"Something in Aurora Beatrix Lane's story must have really struck us," Paulina mused.

"Definitely," Nicky agreed. "Aurora was RESOURCEFUL and **gutsy**, just like us!"

"And she loved to travel, just like we do," Violet added. "It's too bad she never managed to fulfill all her dreams. And it's sad that the ALABASTER GARDEN is destined to remain a mystery."

The five friends all stopped eating at the SAME TIME. It was one of those moments when, without needing to speak, the five of them knew they had had the same idea.

Finally, Pam broke the silence.

"Are the rest of you thinking what I'm thinking?" she asked.

"Let me guess," Colette began with a smile. "You're thinking classes at Mouseford Academy don't start right away . . ."

". . . so we have time to help Beitris figure out who stole the tapestry . . ." Nicky continued.

". . . and help her FIND IT!" Paulina said.

"Don't forget the **ALABASTER GARDEN**," Violet added. "Maybe we can solve that **MYSTERY**, too!"

"So we all agree!" Pam exclaimed. "We should postpone our return flights and start ***investigating***!"

"But where do we begin?" Paulina asked.

"Well, the entire story revolves around one person," Violet said.

"*Aurora Beatrix Lane*!" the others all called out.

Violet nodded.

"I'll do

some research on her," she said. "Even if she didn't **Leave** official records of her trips, maybe we can find other **evidence**."

"Did **Beitris** mention the name of the college in England where Aurora studied?" Paulina asked.

"She did!" Nicky recalled. "It was **GIRTON COLLEGE** at the University of Cambridge!"

"Fantastic!" Pam exclaimed. "All we need to do is pack our bags and go! Well, after we finish breakfast, of course!"

The five mice burst out laughing.

They couldn't wait to start their next adventure!

DESTINATION: CAMBRIDGE

A few hours later, the Thea Sisters were on a train and then a bus to Cambridge. The bus stopped very close to their destination: GIRTON COLLEGE.

"Wow!" Paulina exclaimed as she admired the redbrick building in front of them. "It's amazing to think that Aurora studied right **here** almost a century ago."

"Let's head inside," Violet said. "I called and made an appointment with the dean."

"Welcome!" the dean greeted them warmly.

The Thea Sisters explained that they wanted to research a student who had attended the school years ago, and he proved to be very helpful . . . and very chatty!

CAMBRIDGE, ENGLAND

The city of Cambridge is located in England, about sixty miles from London. The famouse University of Cambridge is one of the oldest universities, and it attracts visitors and students from all over the world. Many famous people have studied there, including mathematician Isaac Newton, naturalist Charles Darwin, and primatologist Dian Fossey.

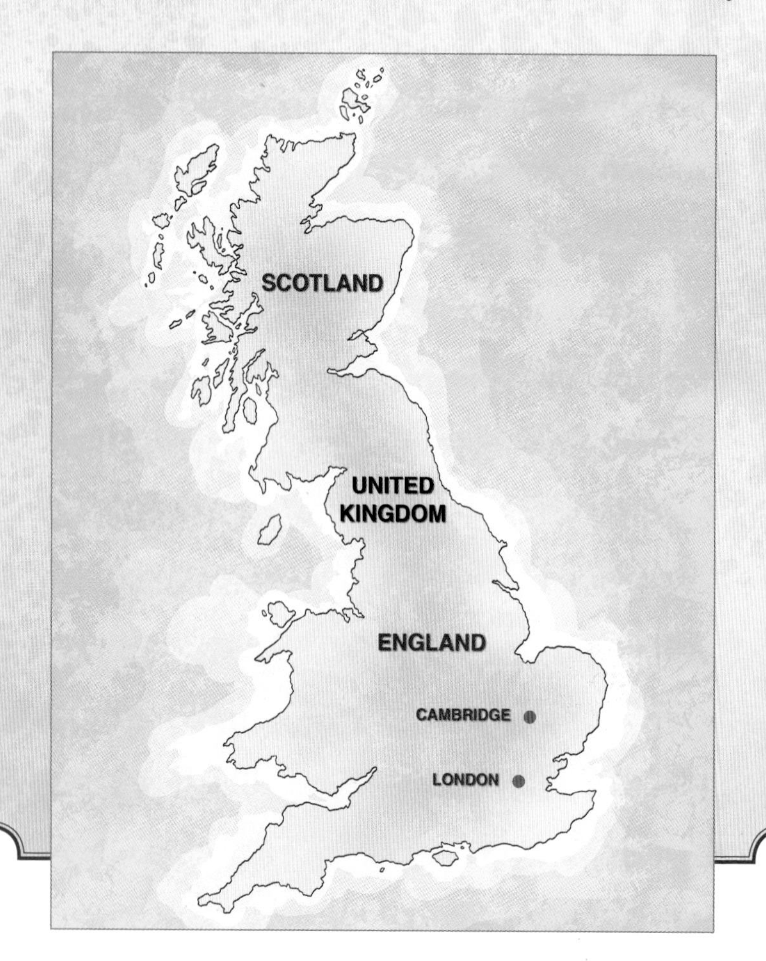

The dean was very interested in giving the Thea Sisters a tour of the college, from the classrooms to the dorm rooms, telling them the history of each place in great **detail**.

"Griton College was founded in 1869, and was originally an all-mouselets school," the dean explained. "The typical **redbrick** architecture is thanks to . . ."

The friends exchanged worried glances as the dean chattered on and on.

"He's just like Headmaster de Mousus," Pam whispered to Violet. "When he starts squeaking he never stops!"

Meanwhile, the dean hadn't heard a thing. He **continued**: "And now we'll enter the great room, which as you can see is a **perfect** example of Victorian architecture . . ."

When the five mice stepped into the room, they were squeakless.

The shiny wood walls and tall, arched windows made it seem like they had stepped back in time.

"**WOW!**" Colette exclaimed. "It's so beautiful."

"Today this room is reserved for events and banquets . . ." the dean continued.

Violet stifled a yawn as she tried to figure out a way to politely **interrupt** the dean.

Finally, he stopped for a moment to catch his **breath**.

Colette took advantage of the opportunity and quickly jumped in.

"Thank you so much for your very **interesting** explanations," she gushed. "We really do need to begin our research. Is it possible for us to consult your **oldest** archives?"

"Oh yes, of course!" the dean replied. "You're looking for information on a **student** who graduated about a hundred years ago, correct? You'll want to try the central archive, but . . ."

"But what?" Colette asked anxiously.

"I'm afraid it's **CLOSED**!" the dean replied.

The friends **LOOKED** at one another in

dismay. Had they come all this way for NOTHING?

Before they could respond, the dean continued. "But you can come back tomorrow when it reopens! I have a meeting first thing in the morning, but my assistant will be able to let you into the ARCHIVE and show you around until I can get there."

The five mice breathed sighs of relief. Then they quickly thanked him for his help and said good-bye before he had a chance to begin squeaking again!

The Thea Sisters headed straight to the bed-and-breakfast where they were staying. They were exhausted from their long day of travel and they couldn't wait to put their paws up and relax!

A SEARCH THROUGH THE PAST

"Rise and shine, Pam!" Colette squeaked to her friend the next morning. Pam was still snuggled under the covers in a **deep sleep**.

"Huh?" she asked groggily as she sat up in bed. "Is it morning **ALREADY**?"

"Yes, and we need to *GET BACK* to Girton College," Colette replied.

Hearing those words, Pam pressed the pillow to her ears.

"Oh no," she groaned. "I don't think I can listen to another one of the dean's long-winded lessons!"

Her **friends** laughed.

"Well, if we get there early enough, he'll still be in his meeting and we can begin

exploring the ARCHIVE on our own, remember?" Violet said.

"You're right," Pam said decisively. She got out of bed and dressed quickly. "Let's go, then! But let's grab breakfast first. I'm so HUNGRY!"

After a DELICIOUS breakfast of muffins and scones, the mouselets found themselves at GIRTON COLLEGE once more. They stood in front of a door that read CENTRAL ARCHIVE, but unfortunately the door was locked and the dean's assistant was NOWHERE to be found!

"Now what do we do?" Pam asked.

Violet sighed. "I guess we'll have to come back later," she squeaked.

Just as the Thea Sisters turned to leave, two blond ratlets appeared at the end of the hallway.

"HELLO!" the first one exclaimed.

"You five are from Mouseford, right? I'm Philip, and this is my brother James."

"Nice to meet you," Colette greeted them. "But how do you know who we are?"

James was the one who shyly explained. "The dean spoke to us about you, and he asked us to come let you into the ARCHIVE."

"But the dean told us we would be meeting his assistant," Violet replied.

"Trouble is, she's on vacation!" Philip smiled. "The dean is a little absentminded, but don't worry . . . he realized his mistake last night and asked us to help you."

"Thanks, that's really kind!" Nicky said.

"It's not a problem," James responded. "Sometimes we help organize things in the archive, so we can help you find the information you need."

A moment later, the mouselets were in a room full of photographs, computers, and leather-bound books.

"What are you looking for exactly?" Philip asked.

"We're researching a student named Aurora Beatrix Lane," Paulina explained. "She graduated about a hundred years ago."

Did you find anything?
There are so many books!

"Okay, then we'll need to consult the HISTORIC ARCHIVE and do some cross-referencing," Philip replied.

"Oh, is that complicated?" Colette asked, concerned.

"A little bit," Philip admitted. "But historic research is our specialty. Modestly squeaking, no one can top us!"

James turned a bit **red**. "Philip, don't brag!" he scolded in a teasing tone. Then he turned to the Thea Sisters. "We'll do our best to help."

The brothers sat down in front of two computers and began to **type** eagerly as the Thea Sisters watched, impressed. They searched through pages and pages of results, and in less than fifteen minutes, Philip cheered.

"FOUND IT!" he exclaimed. "Here's the

announcement that went out when she received her degree . . . along with a **photograph**!"

The Thea Sisters peered at the screen. There they saw a young Aurora smiling proudly while standing next to a tall, skinny mouse with a serious air.

"I think that must be . . ." Paulina began.

"**Professor von Klawitz!**" Nicky exclaimed. She easily recognized the FAMOUSE archaeologist who had been Aurora's teacher.

"Look!" Paulina exclaimed, *pointing* to the image. "Aurora is holding a book . . ."

"It's a JOURNAL!" exclaimed Colette. "See the cover? There's no title, but there are three letters . . . *A*, *B*, and *L*, which stand for . . ."

". . . Aurora Beatrix Lane!" Nicky concluded.

As the Thea Sisters stared at the **photograph**, James cleared his throat to get their attention.

"Umm, I've actually seen these initials here at Girton," he said.

All five friends turned to him at once.

"You have?" Violet asked in disbelief. "Please, tell us more!"

THE PERFECT HIDING PLACE

"You've seen those letters somewhere else here? **Where?!**" Nicky asked.

"It was in the ANCIENT LIBRARY, right, Phil?" James asked his brother.

Philip nodded and then turned to the Thea Sisters. "Come with us," he said.

Then he turned around and began **WALKING** quickly, followed by his brother. The Thea Sisters were a bit **SURPRISED**, but they followed behind them.

"Don't you want to tell us more?" Colette squeaked between breaths. She was having trouble keeping up with the brothers, who were scampering eagerly down the college's long corridors.

"Nah, just wait until we get there," Philip replied. "It's better if we just **show you**!"

Finally, they entered an old room whose walls were partly lined with shelves full of bound volumes. Large windows let in the sun, which lit up the wood floor; the rich, geometrically patterned carpets; and the beautiful stone fireplace.

Philip and James headed straight for the FIREPLACE, of all things.

"This is the Stanley Library," James explained in a quiet voice. "This room and collection dates back to the end of the 1800s . . ."

"Please!" Pam cried, interrupting him. "We got enough history lessons yesterday from the dean!"

James was squeakless for a moment, then laughed.

"You're right," he said. "But you'll want to hear this. You see, we found the initials **ABL** inside the fireplace!"

"**What?!**" Nicky exclaimed in disbelief. "You found them *in* the fireplace?"

"That's right," Philip replied as he ducked his head under the fireplace hood. "A few months ago, it was our friend Bradley's birthday. He always plays pranks on us, so we decided that for once we would play one on him."

He paused for a moment.

"Now **WHERE** was it?" Philip mumbled to himself, feeling around inside the fireplace with his paw.

"We got him a birthday gift," James continued as Philip searched. "But instead of giving it to him directly, we organized a **treasure hunt** throughout the college.

"The idea was for him to follow one clue to the next, eventually finding the gift in a secret hiding spot."

"You mean in this FIREPLACE?" Colette asked in surprise.

"Exactly!" James explained. "And that's where we discovered the initials."

"Here they are!" Phil exclaimed suddenly. "Come take a LOOK!"

The mouselets knelt down in the fireplace, and Nicky slipped in so she could see the place Philip was pointing to.

"It's true!" she cried. "I see it!"

"Wow," Colette murmured dreamily. "That means Aurora was right here in this fireplace a century ago, CARVING her initials in the stone."

"Yes, but why put her initials inside a fireplace?" Violet asked, puzzled. "It doesn't make sense, unless . . ."

"Unless they're *marking* something else," Nicky said suddenly. She began to feel around inside the fireplace near the area with the writing. "Here! There's a spot where the stone is **UNEVEN**. It's just next to the stone with Aurora's initials. Maybe I need to PUSH or PULL . . ."

Suddenly, they all heard a little *click* that **echoed** through the room. The Thea Sisters held their **breath** as Nicky reached up to investigate.

She could feel that a small slab of stone had moved, revealing a

tiny opening in the interior wall of the fireplace. She reached her paw in the opening and pulled something out.

"What is it?" Pam asked eagerly.

"It's **Aurora's journal**!" Colette squeaked, grinning from ear to ear.

Nicky gently removed the small, worn notebook. It had been **well-preserved** inside a metal box, and the friends could clearly read the letters **ABL** on the cover.

Amazing!
What did I tell you?
It's her journal!

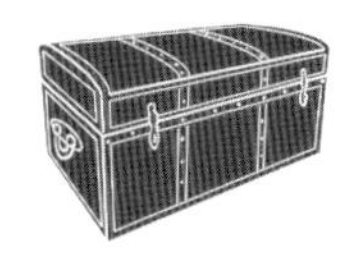

AURORA'S MYSTERY

Nicky delicately held the journal in her paws, as if she were handling a great treasure. Her friends' eyes sparkled with happiness.

"I can't believe it!" Pam squeaked, turning to Philip and James. "We really found it, and it's all THANKS to you two."

"No, you five did everything," James replied.

"Don't be modest!" Pam continued. "Without your help, we never would have looked in this fireplace."

"We're glad to help," Philip said. "But now I'm wondering who this Aurora is, and what CONNECTION she has to you!"

Paulina smiled. "You're right," she said.

"We really should explain everything."

"Aurora was a student at this college, as we told you," Violet began. "She's also the ancestor of a friend of ours, and she's the key to solving a problem our friend is having. Someone took something very important from her. This journal could contain important CLUES on how to get it back!"

Philip and James nodded with understanding.

"Then the best thing for you to do now is to go back to your bed-and-breakfast so you can read it in private among yourselves," James said.

Nicky sighed, clutching the journal to her chest.

"You're absolutely right!" she said. "Let's head back and get to work. We have to figure out what the next step is before those other nasty rodents do."

She couldn't say for sure, but something told her they would find really important information in those pages. She COULDN'T WAIT to read it! Hopefully, it would give the mouselets everything they needed to track down the tapestry.

A short while later, the five friends were gathered together in their room at the bed and breakfast. They sat around Nicky, who prepared herself to read the first pages of the journal **ALOUD**.

ABL

16th of May

Dear Diary,

I have decided to start writing here today, on my first day as a graduate!

The years I spent at Girton College were truly wonderful: I grew up, I made friendships with fantastic mice, and most of all I dedicated myself to archaeology. It is truly my passion, and I will never give it up. This world of ours is full of riches from the past, just waiting to be brought to light.

And I am ready to do that!

The graduation ceremony was yesterday.
I was chosen to give a farewell speech.
My classmates were so excited, but I felt strangely calm. The future sparkles before us, and we just have to give our all to make sure it continues to shine.

While I was on the stage, I looked out at all the relatives who had gathered there for us. My family was all there, including my mom and all six of my sisters.

My mom and all six of my sisters.

For a moment I really felt my dad's absence. But even though he is no longer with us, I always carry him in my heart, and I feel like he has never abandoned me. His voice guides me when I have too many questions inside me, and his hand is still holding mine when things are hard, just like when I was young.

My sister is so sweet! She drew me like this . . .

From the stage I looked at my mom, at Robert, and my sisters. Hannah, Linda, and Susan are already young women, and even Carla is growing up. Petra and Diana, on the other hand, are still little kids. Now I feel like I am the one who must protect and take care of them.

After the ceremony, Professor von Klawitz complimented me on my accomplishments and asked if I would be his assistant on his next few excavations. I am so excited at the thought!

A short while later, I was moved once more when Robert pulled me aside and hugged me, telling me how proud he is of me. This warmed my heart and made the moment even more special.

I am sure that I will always remember this day.

"There's so much **emotion** in her writing," Colette remarked. "I feel as though she was a close friend after hearing just a few pages!"

"Yes, and she was so **ambitious**," Paulina chimed in. "She had so many dreams."

Nicky leafed through the next few pages and summarized them for her friends.

"Here she records her first experiences excavating with **Professor von Klawitz**," Nicky explained. "And then she writes about little Petra's birthday. There's even a photo!"

The Thea Sisters huddled around the journal.

"She really was just like us," Violet remarked. "And learning about her life is ***fascinating***. But we can't forget the **reason** we're doing all this."

"Yes, of course!" Colette agreed. "We need to help Beitris! Vi is right. We should look in the journal for some reference to the **tapestry** or to the **ALABASTER GARDEN**."

"I think I've found something!" Paulina exclaimed. She had taken the journal from Nicky and was leafing through its pages.

23rd of July

Dear Diary,

Professor von Klawitz is unusually nervous these days and is acting very strange.

I have already written about how he is very protective of his trunks, remember?

Well, last night, when I got up to go to the bathroom, I saw that the door to the professor's room was a little bit open. He was standing over an open trunk, contemplating something that looked like a little urn.

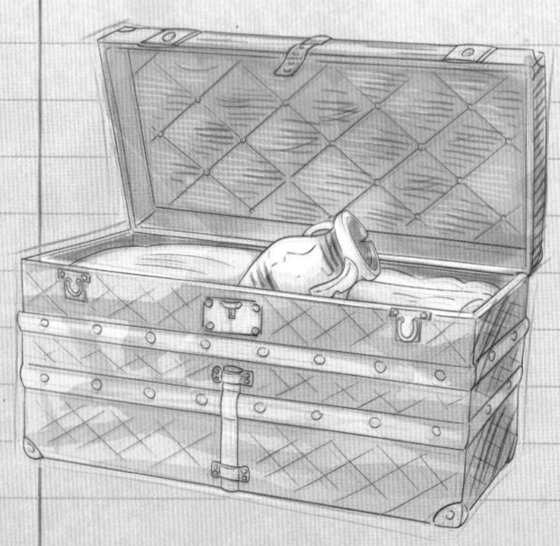

Inside it looked like there was a little urn!

Strange, right? I immediately thought that perhaps he had commissioned some copies of the most beautiful relics he had discovered so that he could bring them with him and study them carefully. But why keep them hidden? It seems like an odd thing to do.

For a moment, I found myself wondering if he had stolen them, but I would never believe it. The professor has too much integrity to do such a thing.

But there was another unusual incident today that I should write about . . .

The day began in the usual way. The professor and the rest of the archaeological team had a long and difficult journey to reach a small village at the top of a hill.

There was a half-ruined castle in an ancient village . . .

The most important building was an old castle that was half in ruins, and, according to the professor, was built on top of the ruins of another ancient structure.

We had already been working for a few hours and I found myself in a room in the castle, happily observing the stucco on the walls. Suddenly, while I was delicately touching one of the walls, I realized that one of the stones moved a little! Curious, I tried to push it, and immediately an underlying panel unlocked. I soon realized it wasn't a simple wall. Rather, it was a hidden door!

Behind the door was a tiny secret room that was covered entirely in mosaic tiles. In the center of the room, there was a lectern, which is a tall stand to hold up books or notes.

I had never seen anything like it!

In the wing of the building where I was working, it was just me and Professor von Klawitz. So I called him and he came at once.

As soon as he saw the secret room, his eyes began to sparkle.

"Aurora, you found it!" he said, darting inside.

The room was very small, but I followed him to find out what he was talking about. On the lectern, there was a tightly bound ancient volume.

I lifted it carefully. Then I began to leaf through the pages, which told of legends and precious treasures. But as I was trying to decipher the Latin title that sparkled in gold on the cover, the professor brusquely grabbed it from my paws.

The ancient book that Klawitz wanted to keep for himself . . .

"I'm taking this!" he said seriously.

I was stunned: The professor has always been kind toward me. Why was he suddenly acting so rudely? And why did he want the book so badly?

Klawitz had never spoken to us about books when he spoke of the possible relics we would uncover at that excavation site.

His strange behavior really struck me.

Then, after a few moments, he returned to his normal self and began explaining that the book was an ancient volume that could be easily damaged, and that it was better if he took it into his care immediately.

When I proposed that I should officially register the discovery of the room and of the book he said that he preferred to do it himself.

It's all very strange, dear Diary: The professor has always been careful to make us follow the proper procedure for all our findings.

Instead, this time he was the one behaving improperly. And he didn't even let me look at the book again.

My father always reminded me that when your instinct tells you something, you should listen.

But what exactly is it in this case? Should I find a way to get more information?

I don't understand . . .

Pam shook her head. "I don't understand what **this** has to do with the stolen tapestry," she said.

"Yeah, how does an old book relate to Beitris and her **problems**?" Nicky asked, confused.

"It may be nothing," Paulina responded, **thoughtful**. "But you heard what Aurora wrote, right? She said the book spoke of **LEGENDS** and **treasures** . . ."

Violet nodded. "Maybe we're on the right track," she said. "Let's try to read a bit more and see if we can **find out**!"

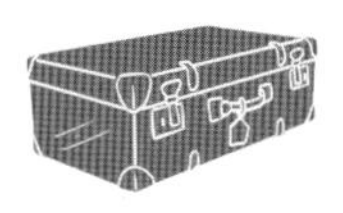

A SECRET IN THE PAGES

Colette and Violet made some tea while Pam prepared a tray of scones she had picked up on the way back from Girton College. Paulina continued to carefully **leaf through** the journal, looking for references to treasures. It didn't take long for her to find something.

"**HERE!**" she exclaimed excitedly.

Nicky had placed some pillows on the carpet, and the friends got comfortable, each one with a **cup** of tea and something to eat.

"We're ready!" Colette said.

"I leafed through some of the pages and I read a bit more," Paulina began.

"Aurora writes about how **Klawitz** acted as if nothing happened after her discovery.

He behaved as though the book didn't even exist!"

"I'm starting not to like this professor so much," Colette commented, scrunching up her snout in disgust.

"Me neither," Paulina agreed. "And Aurora writes that when she asked him questions about the book, he would always respond by changing the topic."

"**So, the plot thickens!**" Nicky exclaimed.

"It's getting quite interesting . . . Yum . . ." Pam replied, her mouth full. "Are you going to eat those?" She pointed to a tray of cookies that Nicky had set down next to her.

Violet giggled. "Concentrate, Pam," she teased. "We might be unraveling a **GREAT MYSTERY**!"

"Let's hope," said Paulina before she continued reading.

Nicky, are you going to eat those?
Concentrate, Pam!

13th of August

Dear Diary,

Yesterday I made a decision. We left the camp to head toward England.

Klawitz had his trunks and all his belongings with him, but during the train trip he met one of his old collaborators. The mouse invited Klawitz to the dining car, leaving me alone in the train compartment with our luggage.

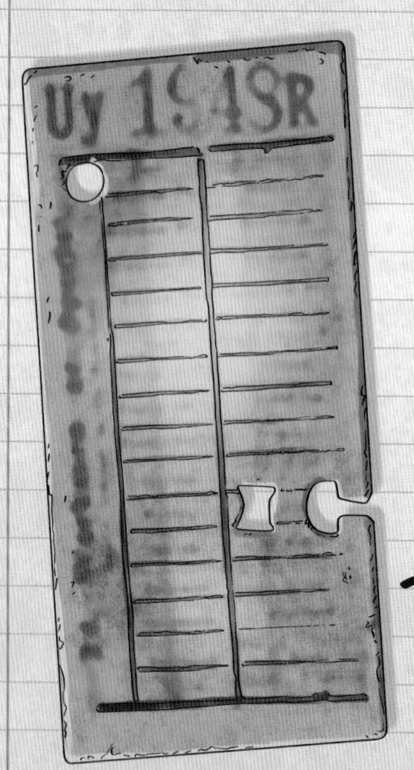

I've saved my train ticket . . .

While I was getting my bag to look at some notes, I accidentally knocked into the professor's trunk. Strangely, the lid wasn't closed. That's how I saw a book inside, and I recognized it at once: It was an elegant blue volume with a golden title — it was the one I had found in the ruined castle!

Now I had proof that the professor hadn't logged and archived the discovery along with the other relics. Instead, he had kept it with his personal belongings. In that moment I decided to take a look inside the book. I wanted to get to the bottom of whatever was going on. It was my duty as an archaeologist to make sure that every finding was made public and wasn't hidden or used for personal reasons.

So, I delicately pulled the book from the trunk. Then I sat down, and, looking briefly at the door to the compartment so I wouldn't be surprised by anyone, I began to read.

The first page had a kind of introduction that went like this:

We know the Seven Wonders of the World, passed down by the Romans and the Greeks.

But only the wisest of the wise know of a greater marvel: the Seven Treasures of the World.

Seven legendary treasures, hidden from those who might profit from them, are hidden in mysterious places all around the world.

Only these pages contain the secret of the seven treasures and their hiding places.

Prepare yourself, reader, to discover the greatest mystery of our world.

As soon as I read those lines, dear Diary, a chill of pure emotion came over me.

What greater dream for an archaeologist than to find the greatest ancient treasures of the world?

I know it seems incredible – and unbelievable. It could just be a legend. Yet was it possible that Klawitz would risk his reputation and his career for an old legend? I don't think so.

I knew the book was something special. I just had to look at its pages to be sure. I don't think it's a legend at all.

I believe the treasures really exist!

"Aurora writes about the legend of the treasures. I'm sure the alabaster garden in the **tapestry** is one of them!" Colette said.

"I know it's late and we're all getting sleepy, but I want to find out more, don't you?" Paulina asked with determination.

The friends all agreed. They were all so intrigued by the **ANCIENT LEGEND** Aurora had discovered that they had to continue reading . . .

IN THE ENEMY'S DEN

Meanwhile, halfway across the world, a moose ambled slowly through a GRASSY meadow dotted with tiny purple flowers, the profile of Denali rising in the distance. As the moose approached a small hill, the earth suddenly began to tremble. The animal trotted away while a metallic platform EMERGED from the small hill, a tiny airplane sparkling on top. A moment later, the airplane lifted up and flew off, disappearing in the Alaskan sky.

The metallic platform retracted and the mysterious trapdoor **closed**. Immediately, it was covered in a layer of artificial grass, and the area was once again a **peaceful** plot of

land in Denali National Park. Deep underground, a long, METALLIC corridor led from the trapdoor to a secret base.

In the base, there was a bedroom, a bathroom, a dining

room, and a laboratory packed with sophisticated high-tech equipment.

There was a large desk in the center of the lab. A mysterious mouse sat there, facing a wall of screens monitoring locations all around the world.

One screen showed the airplane that

had just departed. It was carrying robotic drones that were programmed to fly over and videotape the most remote and mysterious corners of the world.

The screen suddenly FLICKERED and a new image appeared. It showed a young mouse wearing sunglasses and a large, dark-colored hat.

"So, Cassidy?" the mouse at the desk asked GRUFFLY. "Do you have a report for me?"

"Yes, sir," the mouse on the screen replied briskly. "Our experts analyzed the tapestry, but they were not able to decipher the message. Apparently, the rhyme speaks of flower petals and friends with deep feet. It seems to be a DEAD END. We didn't find any useful directions that lead to the treasure."

The mouse at the desk growled and pounded his fist.

"I need you to TRY HARDER, Cassidy!" he squeaked. "There must be some clue in that tapestry. Did you **interrogate** the Scottish mouse? Are you sure she doesn't know anything else?"

"Um, there was a slight **change of plans**,"

Cassidy replied, looking uncomfortable. "The old mouse had some friends show up. We thought it was best to leave at once rather than **risk everything**."

"What friends?" the mouse at the desk demanded.

"There were — uh — five young mice," Cassidy said meekly. "They came from NOWHERE!"

"Well, **WHO** are they?" the mouse at the desk shouted. "**WHERE** did they come from? I want answers!"

"I'm afraid we don't know," Cassidy replied. "The most **IMPORTANT** thing is that we got the tapestry . . ."

"A tapestry that is of no use if we don't understand what it means!" the mouse thundered angrily.

"You've been incredibly **sloppy** in your work, Cassidy."

"I—I'm sorry," the mouse on the screen stuttered in reply.

"You better find those five mice!" the mouse demanded. "They may have some information. I want to know **WHO** they are and **WHAT** they know immediately!"

FURTHER COMPLICATIONS

The Thea Sisters continued to read through Aurora's **journal**, getting more and more interested in her story.

"Does she say anything else about the **treasures**?" Pam asked, trying to peek at the book over Paulina's shoulder.

"Hmmm," Paulina murmured. "Oh! I just found another **PAGE** that seems important . . ."

21st of September

Dear Diary,

Today I gathered my courage and confronted Professor von Klawitz.

Since I found out about the legend of the seven treasures, something in me has changed.

I feel a calling to search for the treasures and to make sure the world knows of their existence. They are riches that belong to everyone, and that everyone should have the right to admire.

So I've gone to the local libraries to expand my research. I even checked the other, farther away, more-equipped ones, to see if there were documents available somewhere that made reference to this legend. For a long time, my investigation was fruitless. But just when I was starting to despair, I had a breakthrough. A dear friend who owns an antique bookstore in Paris mentioned an ancient travel book to me.

The volume references the seven treasures of the earth, held in various places around the world, shrouded in mystery.

I couldn't believe it! Now I finally have a clue that might allow me to fulfill my dream: bringing these hidden treasures to light!

That's why I had to confront the professor: I wanted to propose that we continue to carry out this research together. I knew it wouldn't be easy since he had chosen to keep the story of the legend a secret. But I assumed he was organizing an expedition already and that he hadn't told me because he didn't want a young person without much experience on his team.

But his reaction when I spoke with him was beyond what I ever could have imagined. I had expected him to reject my proposal – at least initially. But I never dreamed he would become so furious when I confessed that I had looked at the book. After all, he knew I was aware of its existence since we had discovered it together. He told me I didn't have the right to look through his things, and he called me a snoop!

You can imagine, dear Diary, how surprised I was!

In all my years studying and working with the well-regarded professor, I've never known him to be so short-tempered and rude!

After a moment, he calmed down a bit and told me that I should forget about the whole thing.

I told him that I wouldn't do that, and he responded that he planned to enjoy the treasures by himself. He had no intention of revealing them to the world.

Dear Diary, I was shocked. I know now that his goals are very different from my own.

Unfortunately, behind the façade of a serious professor lies that of a selfish, greedy, and

unscrupulous collector!

A DREAM TO FULFILL

Paulina closed the journal carefully. As she and her friends read the pages of Aurora's book, they had discovered that the relationship between Aurora and **Professor von Klawitz** soured quickly over their differing views on the legend of the seven treasures. They were both fascinated by the story and the idea of the treasures, but for very different reasons.

The professor wanted to FIND the treasures so he could enrich his personal collection. Aurora's interest, on the other hand, stemmed from the simple desire to return those lost marvels to the world. In the end, Aurora decided to look for the first of the treasures, the **ALABASTER GARDEN**. But the diary ended before she revealed what it was and where it was hidden.

"You know, the mystery of the treasures is **incredible**, but what struck me most is Aurora's integrity," Paulina said. "She really was an extraordinary young mouse."

"You're right," Violet agreed. "She was passionate about **archaeology**, and she also had a strong sense of *right* and **wrong**."

"Yes, she was incredibly **courageous**," Pam added.

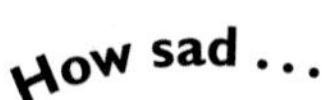

"It's too bad her life ended so mysteriously," Paulina said sadly.

The mouselets were quiet for a moment as they all recalled what they had learned at Beitris's house:

Aurora Beatrix Lane had disappeared aboard her biplane, and to this day, no one knew what had happened to her.

Suddenly, Pamela had a realization.

"Sisters, I think we should continue her adventure!" she squeaked.

"What are you talking about?" Violet asked, intrigued.

"We can be the ones to fulfill her dream," Pam explained. "If we can find the **ALABASTER GARDEN**, we can make sure it's safe! Just think: If the seven precious treasures really do exist and no one today knows it because of Aurora's disappearance, it's a loss for the entire world. We need to do something about it!"

"Pam's right," Nicky said slowly as she thought things through. "We're already involved in the story, and now we have

We should look for the treasure!
For Aurora!

Aurora's notebook, which was hidden for almost a hundred years. We can't turn back now: We need to honor Aurora's memory!"

"And our work could help Beitris solve the mystery of the tapestry," Paulina added.

"The DISHONEST mice who stole the tapestry probably know the legend and are searching for clues to the treasure as we squeak," Violet mused.

"So we'll need to be **faster** than them!" Pamela said.

Colette jumped out of her chair suddenly.

"Well, what are we WAITING for, Sisters?" she squeaked. "**LET'S GET MOVING!**"

"Um, Coco," Nicky said gently, "there are two problems. First, we have no idea where to begin—"

"I think we should go back to Beitris,"

Colette cut in quickly. "I want to make sure she's okay, and we could tell her about the journal. She'll want to see it, and she also might be able to help us."

"I think that's a GREAT idea," Violet agreed.

"But you're forgetting the second problem," Nicky said. "It's almost two in the morning. We have to get some sleep before we hit the road!"

The others burst out laughing.

"Okay, okay," Colette agreed with a yawn. "Tomorrow we'll say good-bye to James and Philip and thank them for their help. Then we'll be on our way back to Scotland!"

A NEW LEAD

The next morning, the Thea Sisters woke up early and returned to GIRTON COLLEGE to find James and Philip and to say good-bye.

"Wow . . . what an adventure!" James remarked when the Thea Sisters had filled him and his brother in on their plans.

"I would really love to come with you five!" Philip exclaimed. "If only we didn't have EXAMS right around the corner."

"Don't worry," Paulina said. "We understand completely. We wouldn't be so free ourselves if we didn't have an extra-long vacation from **MOUSEFORD ACADEMY** this year!"

The brothers were sorry to see the Thea Sisters go.

Then James lit up. "We can do one thing, though," he said. "We can take you to the station!"

"Right!" Philip agreed.

The Thea Sisters accepted the offer gratefully. In no time, the Thea Sisters were READY to leave.

"Good-bye Philip! Good-bye James!" Paulina called, once they arrived at the station. "Thanks for everything!"

"We were glad to help," James replied.

"Yes, good luck!" Philip added.

So, the Thea Sisters returned to Scotland. But when they arrived at Beitris's house, they noticed that the front door was damaged and a window was BROKEN.

"Oh no," Pam said. "I hope Beitris is okay!"

Anxiously, the mice rushed to the front door and began knocking loudly.

"Beitris!" Nicky called out. "Are you here? Are you okay?"

After a moment their friend came to the window.

"I'm not so young anymore, but luckily I can still hear quite well," she said with a chuckle. "*Welcome back!*"

"Sorry," Nicky said sheepishly. "We were just so worried."

"What happened?" Violet asked with concern.

Beitris replied by gesturing for them to sit down. Then she went into the kitchen.

The five friends tried to wait patiently, but they were eager to know what was going on.

Finally, Beitris returned and began to set

the wood table. She placed a pitcher of **juice** in the middle.

"Those thugs **returned** two days ago," she explained.

"What?!" Paulina exclaimed. "They didn't hurt you, did they?"

Beitris shook her head. "I'll admit that they

surprised me," she said calmly. "But not enough to stop me from driving them off with a few swings of my broom!"

Colette couldn't hold back a giggle. "That must have been a sight!" she exclaimed.

"But what did they **WANT**?" Violet asked, worried. "They already have your tapestry. Why return and **RISK** getting caught? Do you have other objects here that are tied to Aurora?"

"No," Beitris replied, shaking her head. "This time they weren't looking for something, but **SOMEONE**. In fact, they were looking for the **five of you**."

The mouselets **LOOKED** at one another, baffled.

"They kept asking me questions about who you are and what you have to do with Aurora," Beitris continued. "Naturally, I didn't tell them a thing. They left when I made them believe the police were coming, and that my FIERCE dog would help me kick them out."

As if she was following our conversation, the sweet dog, who was curled up under the table, gave a little whimper.

"Well, we're glad you're OKAY," Paulina reflected. "But I don't like the sound of this."

"We have to figure out who these THUGS are!" Colette added.

"Yes," Violet agreed seriously. "The only thing we know is that they want to get their paws on the treasure that the tapestry talks about."

"And luckily now we have a new source of information," Nicky chimed in as she

removed a PACKAGE from her backpack and handed it to Beitris.

"What's this?" Beitris asked, a confused look on her snout. She opened the package and looked at it in disbelief. Then her eyes lit up with emotion.

"I can't believe it," she whispered. "It's Aurora's journal!"

It's Aurora's journal!

A FORGOTTEN LETTER

While Beitris flipped through the journal, Nicky told her what they had discovered. "In it, Aurora talks about a **LEGEND** that is linked to seven precious treasures spread throughout the world," she explained. "We think one of those treasures is the **ALABASTER GARDEN**. Unfortunately, some of the pages are missing, and the information in the diary is incomplete."

Beitris was quiet and **thoughtful** for a moment.

"Perhaps I can help," she said finally. "I have something else to **SHOW** you."

She stood and went to a nearby shelf. Then she climbed a stepladder and reached up, pulling down an engraved **WOODEN** box. She stepped down from the ladder and opened the box, removing a yellowed envelope.

"This is the letter Aurora gave my grandmother Petra along with the tapestry," she explained. "For my grandmother, the disappearance of her beloved older sister was a real tragedy. That's also one of the reasons the tapestry was so important to her: It was a memory of Aurora."

"Don't worry, Beitris," Nicky said confidently. "We'll ***find*** the tapestry and **solve** this mystery. I promise!"

Beitris nodded and gave her the letter.

Dear Petra, my beloved little sister,

Your explorer sister is leaving you with an important task.

This package contains a very special tapestry. I can't tell you much but know that it leads to a hidden treasure. I will come back to get it when the time is right: meanwhile, please take very good care of it. A long time may pass before you see me again, but you must trust me. I can count on you, right, my dear one? One day I will tell you everything, but for now I must go. Think of me often. I leave you with a big kiss and an even bigger hug.

Your loving sister,
Aurora

PS If you ever need help, trust only Robert.

"It's a touching letter," Colette commented. "But unfortunately, it doesn't give us too many clues."

"The Robert she speaks of is the doctor that Aurora had a special friendship with, right?" Violet asked.

"Exactly," Beitris confirmed.

"So maybe he had some answers . . ." Violet mused.

Robert, a good friend

"Perhaps, but he, too, is no longer with us," Beitris replied with another sigh.

Everyone was quiet for a moment. Then Beitris gave a sudden start.

"But of course!"

she exclaimed. "How come I didn't think of it before?"

"What is it?" Nicky asked in excitement.

"Robert had a nephew he was very close to named John," Beitris explained. "One time I went to visit him with my grandmother. He had just moved to Brittany, France, to be a lighthouse keeper. Naturally he will be quite old by now, but you should be able to reach him. Let me check to see if I have any more information . . ."

Beitris went over to a desk that was in the corner of the room. She opened it and pulled out a small notebook. Then she flipped through a few pages.

"Ah, yes!" she exclaimed. "Here it is! John Neville lives in Brittany, on the Île de Sein, to be precise. What do you think of going to visit him?"

"That's a great idea!" Paulina replied happily. "But are you sure you're okay staying here by yourself?"

"I know how to look after myself," Beitris replied with a chuckle. "And the police station isn't far away. Plus, now that I know the five of you are working to solve Aurora's mystery, I feel calmer. I'm so grateful for your help!"

The Thea Sisters SMILED. They couldn't think of anything they would rather do than help their friend solve the fascinating mystery of Aurora and the treasure of the ALABASTER GARDEN.

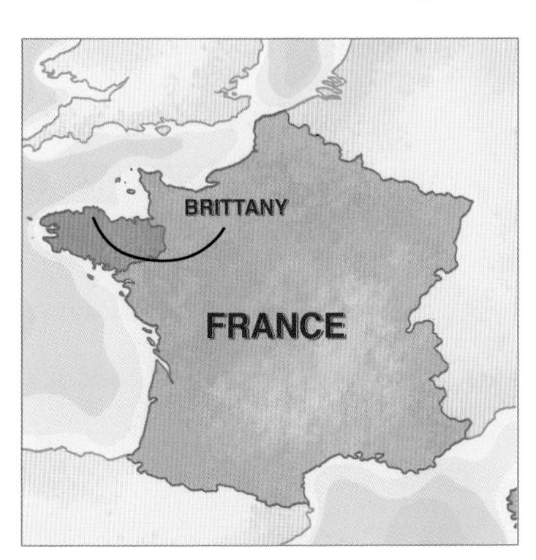

OFF TO FRANCE!

A few hours later, the Thea Sisters were on a plane to France.

"This constant traveling is exhausting!" Violet said with a big yawn.

Colette, who was sitting next to her on the plane, smiled. "You're right, Vi, but I'm so **EXCITED** to be headed home to **France**, I don't care about being tired!"

"Coco, if you want to take advantage of the trip to go visit your family in Paris, you should," Paulina chimed in. "You can always ***catch up*** with us later."

But Colette shook her head. "Don't even think of it," she said. "I wouldn't miss one second of this adventure. And anyway, I called my parents from Scotland. They're meeting us at the airport in Paris and they'll drive us to Brittany!"

"How wonderful!" Pam exclaimed. "You'll get to see your family, and we'll save a lot of time and energy."

"Did you tell your parents the reason for our trip, though?" Paulina asked.

Colette shook her head. "I said I was taking a trip with my very best friends and that I would explain it when I saw them."

Half an hour later, the plane landed at Charles de Gaulle Airport in Paris. Colette darted for the exit: Her parents were among the crowds of people waiting, and they wrapped her in a very sweet hug.

Colette's friends were glad she was so happy, but seeing Colette with her parents made the other Thea Sisters think of their

It's so great to see you!
Welcome home!

own families so far away. For a moment, a bit of sadness fell over everyone as they thought about how much they missed their families.

But once Colette and her mother began chatting, the mood lightened.

"Since there are seven of us, I rented a van," Colette's father told them as the group walked together to the parking lot.

"We hope you haven't gone out of your way too much," Violet said apologetically.

"**It's no trouble at all!**" Colette's father replied. "It's not every day that we have our Colette here in France, and it's even rarer for her to bring her four **best friends** with her! It's the least we could do."

Colette's mom rummaged through her purse. She pulled out a tiny package and gave it to Colette.

"*Mon chou**, here's a little gift for you: a travel manicure kit!"

"Thank you!" Colette said, happily giving her mom a big hug. "You're the BEST mom ever!"

By this time, they had reached the van.

"Okay, everyone climb in!" Colette's dad said cheerfully. "We should leave right away if we want to reach Brittany before nightfall!"

* In French, this is an affectionate way to say "sweetie."

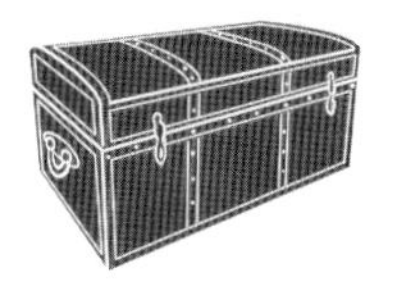

IN BRITTANY AT LAST

After a few hours, the group finally reached **Brittany**. The Thea Sisters' destination was the ***Île de Sein***, an island off the westernmost coast of France, in Brittany.

They stopped in the port town of Audierne. As the five friends climbed out of the van, they could smell the **SEA AIR** all around them.

"You'll love Brittany," Colette's mother told them. "It's a beautiful part of France that has managed to preserve a lot of its **ancient culture**."

"Yes, but before we discuss French history, let's eat!" Colette's father exclaimed. "I don't know about the rest of you, but I'm hungry.

What do you say we head to a **restaurant** for some dinner?"

Pamela nodded gratefully, her stomach rumbling. "That sounds fabumouse."

"Dad, you're right," Colette agreed. "The best thing we can do now is **eat**, find a place

to stay, and get a good night's rest."

"We can continue our mission first thing tomorrow morning," Violet added.

"A MISSION for school, right?" Colette's mother asked.

"Well, not exactly . . ." her daughter replied. "We're on the TRAIL of a pilot who lived almost a century ago!"

Her parents were curious about the story, so on their way to dinner, Colette and her friends told them about Aurora Beatrix Lane, Beitris, and the stolen tapestry.

"We found her journal in Cambridge, and it made us want to track down more information about the treasures she was searching for," Paulina explained.

"We think the criminals who stole the tapestry are probably doing the same thing," Violet added.

Colette's father became **VERY SERIOUS**. "I think that what you're doing is noble, but please be very careful," he said.

But Colette's mom smiled confidently at the five friends.

"*Mon chérie**, you know our Colette can look after herself," she told her husband. "And she has her amazing friends with her! I just know they'll solve the mystery and honor Aurora's memory. And at the first sign of **DANGER**, they know to call the authorities."

"Of course, Mom!" Colette agreed. "Don't worry!"

The group had walked across town, and they now found themselves in front of a lovely restaurant. As soon as they were seated, Colette suggested some typical French dishes to her friends. By the time the food

*In French, this means "my dear."

arrived at the table, everyone was ready to eat.

Colette was thrilled to be spending the evening with her parents, and her friends were equally happy and enjoying the meal as well. That is, except for **Violet**.

"I don't know why, but I feel **uneasy**," she whispered to Paulina. "I almost feel as though someone is **WATCHING** us."

Paulina glanced around the restaurant. "But who could be watching us?" she asked. "No one even knows we're here."

"You're right," Violet said, sighing. She picked up her fork and kept eating, trying to ignore the feeling of **uneasiness** that had come over her.

Huh?
I feel uneasy!

A LEGENDARY LIGHTHOUSE

After spending the night in a delightful hotel, the Thea Sisters said good-bye to Colette's parents the next morning. They had to return to Paris for work.

"Be careful!" her dad called out from the van in a fatherly tone as he pulled away.

"Now where do we **START**, sisters?" Pam asked.

"According to the research I did on my tablet, John was the **keeper** for Ar-Men, a lighthouse off the *Île de Sein* . . ." Paulina began.

"Was?" Nicky asked, confused.

Paulina nodded. "The lighthouse was automated more than twenty-five years ago,"

she explained. "I did some internet searches, but I couldn't find any information about what happened to John then."

"Well, first we need to go to Ar-Men and LOOK there," Nicky said. "Let's take the ferry."

The five friends headed straight for the port. As they sailed across the open waters toward the Île de Sein, they hypothesized about where they might find John.

Colette was the only one who remained silent.

"Coco, are you all right?" Paulina asked. "Are you tired?"

"No," Colette replied, shaking her head.

"Do you miss your parents?" Violet asked sweetly. "I know I would."

Colette shook her head once more.

"What is it, then?" Pam asked, concerned.

"**I'M SEASICK!**" Colette exclaimed.

"I thought your fur looked a bit **green**," Pam remarked.

"The sea is pretty **rough**," Violet said as she took in the **DARK** sky. "Try looking at the **horizon**. Sometimes focusing on something steady helps."

"Thanks," Colette groaned.

"We'll be there soon," Paulina said. "**Stay strong!**"

"Actually, we're already here!" Nicky called out. "It's the *Île de Sein*!"

A marina appeared in front of the Thea Sisters, a line of picturesque little houses dotting the shore. Once they got off the ferry, the friends questioned a port worker, who POINTED out the Ar-Men lighthouse.

"Wow," Nicky murmured. "Life as the lighthouse keeper there must have been tough."

"Yes, it was," said a voice behind them suddenly. "It was solitary and difficult, but also exciting."

The Thea Sisters turned to find an old mouse with a WHITE BEARD and two piercing blue eyes.

It looks like rain!
There's the lighthouse!

"But why are you five youngsters so interested in a DANGEROUS old lighthouse?" he asked.

"We're actually looking for one of the former keepers," Colette explained. "His name was John. Do you know him?"

"Why are you looking for him?" he asked.

The friends exchanged looks: They couldn't reveal their entire mission. Could they trust him?

"We need to ask him a few QUESTIONS," Paulina said at last.

"You want to know what life was like down there, right?" the mouse replied, pointing to the lighthouse.

Colette was about to protest, but the mouse sat down on a bench and beckoned the five of them closer.

The friends couldn't help but gather around

as he began to squeak.

"You know, the keeper sometimes used to spend up to three months completely isolated in that lighthouse when the STORMS were bad," he said. "Three months in the middle of the SEA, without squeaking to anyone except by radio. The keeper had the task of keeping the light glowing for ships, sometimes while a storm made the walls shake so much it seemed like the lighthouse was about to collapse and crumble into the sea!"

The Thea Sisters glanced at one another. They all had the same thought.

"Are you . . ." Violet began.

"John?" the man replied with a chuckle. "Yes, you've GUESSED it. That's me!"

THE AR-MEN LIGHTHOUSE

The Ar-Men lighthouse was completed in 1881, though work began in 1867. It is located on the westernmost rock of the Chaussée de Sein, a large area of reefs off the coast of the Île de Sein. The Chaussée de Sein is known for its rough and dangerous waters. The structure's isolated position and extreme conditions meant the builders could only work when the tide was low and the sea was calm. Dangerous storms often prevented keepers at Ar-Men from being relieved at the end of their thirty-day shifts, so longer shifts were common.

Bringing Back Memories

The Thea Sisters couldn't believe their luck: They had easily found Robert's nephew, John. But John still thought they were interested in the life of a lighthouse keeper.

"Being isolated in the middle of the sea could be lonely and frightening, especially in the middle of a **POWERFUL** storm," John continued wistfully. "But there were also days when dawn on the ocean was so *perfect* I felt like the luckiest mouse on Earth!"

"Umm . . . we . . ." Colette tried to interject, but John stopped her, gesturing with his paw.

"I know, I know, these are the stories of an old chatterbox," he said nostalgically. "Now that all the lighthouses are **automated**, old keepers like me are a forgotten bunch. But you probably want to see some **photographs** instead of listening to me blabber on and on. Or perhaps you'd like to see some of the instruments of the trade. **Come to my house!**"

With those words, John got up and started moving. The Thea Sisters decided to follow.

They walked along an unpaved ***path*** that went up a hill.

"Maybe it will be easier to talk to him at his house," Nicky commented under her breath as she

Young John and the lighthouse

This is my house!
How beautiful!

followed the determined steps of the old lighthouse keeper.

"We'll be safe as long as we are together. And maybe he'll have some memory of Robert and Aurora!" Colette added confidently.

John's house was surrounded by fields and rocks and had a fabumouse view of the isolated Ar-Men lighthouse. The air smelled distinctly of the SEA.

"Please make yourselves **comfortable**," John said as he gestured for the Thea Sisters to enter.

Inside, the house was sparsely furnished: There was a table with WOODEN benches, round windows like portholes, and a simple bed in the corner. John opened a drawer and took out some NOTEBOOKS and some nautical calculation instruments.

"These are my memories from that time in my life," he explained.

"Did you keep any journals?" Nicky asked, looking at the books.

John nodded. "It's a habit that I picked up from a special mouse I met when I was very young. Every day she would record her adventures and her discoveries . . ."

"Was her name Aurora, by any chance?" Colette asked.

John jumped in surprise. "**How did you know?!**" he asked, shocked.

"We have this," Nicky said, pulling Aurora's journal out of her bag.

John took it and

held it gently in his paws without squeaking.

After a long pause, he whispered: "Who are you? Why are you here?"

In a few short words, Nicky told him the whole story. She explained how they had met Aurora's great-niece Beitris by chance. Nicky also told John about the ancient tapestry and the theft.

She concluded the tale by explaining how she and her friends had been so struck by Aurora's story that they were now following her tracks in an effort to help their Scottish friend.

"Beitris . . . of course I remember her!" John said. "She was a tiny mouse with **bright blue** eyes. Her grandmother Petra adored her."

The Thea Sisters nodded. All the strands of the story were finally beginning to **COME**

TOGETHER, and the hope of learning more was becoming a certainty.

"We went to Girton College in England, where Aurora had been a student," Violet explained. "We found this journal there. The journal mentions a treasure tied to the stolen tapestry, but it ends without revealing any more details."

"We know that the only one Aurora trusted was Robert," Colette continued. "And Beitris told us that he had a nephew he was very close to."

"You're one of our last hopes!" Paulina squeaked. "We came here hoping to find out more about Aurora and the mystery of the lost treasures."

John took a small photograph from one of the notebooks.

"It's from years ago," he said.

Aurora, Robert, and little John

"WHY, THAT'S AURORA!" Pam exclaimed, pointing to the smiling pilot in the photograph.

John sighed, and his expression softened.

"She was a wonderful mouse," he squeaked. "She was courageous and full of life. I was very small when she disappeared . . . it was many, many years ago! Yet I remember her as if it were yesterday. She would always say:

'John, don't ever forget how important it is to follow your dreams!'"

"What a beautiful message," Colette commented, smiling.

"I think it was thanks to that advice that I never hesitated to follow my own dreams," John remarked. "That's how I ended up as a lighthouse keeper in the middle of the ocean. I've always loved the SEA, and being close to the wind, waves, and the salt air has always been my greatest desire."

John had a dreamy look in his eyes and he seemed LOST in his memories. But a second later he snapped back to the present day.

"I'm ready to help you however I can," he said. "Aurora's memory should be honored. Ask me whatever you like."

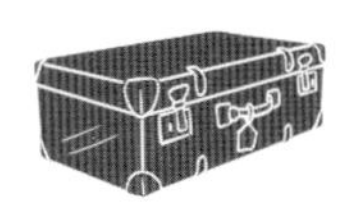

A CHAIN OF MYSTERIES

The Thea Sisters were eager to hear more: Perhaps John's tale could give them a new **CLUE** that would help them in their search.

"Can you can tell us anything about the **tapestry**?" Paulina asked hopefully.

John thought quietly for a moment, but then he shook his head.

"I'm afraid I don't know anything about the tapestry," he explained. "My first memories of Aurora and my uncle Robert are that they were **BEST FRIENDS**, though I suspect they were much more, even if my uncle never told me that."

"It must have been hard for him when Aurora **disappeared**," Colette remarked.

John nodded. "I was young, but I remember that it was a **terrible time** for him. For years he led searches in the area where Aurora and her professor **disappeared**, but no one ever found anything."

"Aurora and her professor?!" Nicky exclaimed. "You mean **Professor von Klawitz**?"

"Yes, that name sounds right," John said. "They disappeared in the **same place**, at the **SAME TIME**, during a terrible storm. But they were on two different planes. The details were never clear, but I don't think they were getting along well at the time. Some people thought they were involved in a ***chase*** on that day."

Violet felt her fur stand on end.

"Aurora disappeared years after she wrote about her suspicions of **Klawitz** in her

journal," she reflected.

"Is it possible that the conflict between Aurora and her professor went on for so many years?" Colette asked.

"It could be," John replied. "But that's just a guess. Uncle Robert didn't talk to me about Aurora after she disappeared. I think the memories were just too painful for him."

"That's understandable," Colette said sympathetically.

"In my time **alone** at the lighthouse, one of my favorite pastimes was researching Aurora and her discoveries," John continued. "In addition to being my uncle's **closest friend**, she was a fascinating mouse. I wanted to know as much as possible about her."

John removed a different notebook from a **drawer**. It was thicker, and there were

A. B. LANE AND J. VON KLAWITZ ON THEIR LAST FLIGHT

SEPTEMBER – Aurora Beatrix Lane, known for her archaeological and exploratory endeavors, was on board her aircraft when a storm broke out. She has not been heard from since. Cambridge professor Jan von Klawitz disappeared under the same circumstances. Klawitz had been Lane's professor in the past, and according to some, was in competition with his former student.

newspaper clippings and tickets of all kinds in it.

"That's it!" Pam cried after she had seen the newspaper article in John's notebook. "Aurora and her professor disagreed about the seven treasures."

"The **seven treasures**?" John asked.

"In her journal, Aurora wrote about finding

an ancient **book** that contained a legend about seven treasures hidden in seven secret places throughout the world," Violet explained.

"Aurora and Klawitz had **different ideas** about the treasures," Nicky continued. "She wanted to share them with the world, while he selfishly wanted to keep them in his own private collection."

John smiled. "Everything makes sense now," he said. "You know, Aurora was a very unique **archaeologist**. She didn't want to study just one time period or style. Instead, she chose to travel the world, uniting her **love** for archaeology with adventure and **EXPLORATION**. And guess how many trips she went on looking for artifacts?"

"**Seven!**" the Thea Sisters cried in unison.

"Exactly," John replied. "So we just have to

find out the destinations of each of the **seven trips**."

"The first trip should lead to the **ALABASTER GARDEN**," Paulina mused. "If we can get there before the crooks who stole

the tapestry, maybe we can prevent the treasure from falling into the wrong paws!"

John shook his head. "That would be perfect," he agreed. "But there's one **BIG** problem: I haven't managed to reconstruct Aurora's **EXACT DESTINATIONS**. It seems incredible, but she really knew how to keep nearly all her research secret. And now I understand why."

"She didn't want **Klawitz** to get in the way of her plans," Violet concluded.

"Wait a second . . ." John said as he leafed through another stack of diaries and notebooks. "**YES!** Here it is!"

The old mouse showed the Thea Sisters a newspaper clipping that was a bit faded, but the title was clear:

"The young archaeologist Aurora Beatrix Lane heads to Mexico."

Underneath the headline was the **faded** text of an interview.

"**Mexico** . . ." Violet reflected. "The treasure that we're looking for could **be there**! All we have to do is pack our bags and book a flight!"

UNDERGROUND INTRIGUE

Meanwhile, in the depths of his bunker under Alaska's Denali National Park, a sinister mouse was nervously pacing his laboratory. So far, nothing was going according to his **PLAN**. As soon as he had reconstructed the legend of the seven treasures, he had been determined to find them. The only one who had left any useful **TRACES** of the treasures was Aurora Beatrix Lane.

Yet all his research had come to nothing! He was used to getting exactly what he wanted whenever he wanted it. To clear his head, he decided to do what he loved best: **admire** his collection of priceless rare artifacts. His **great-grandfather** had started the collection, and ever since his own childhood, he had been determined to complete it in any way possible.

He approached a **METALLIC** door and entered a code on the **keypad** on the wall. The door opened with a **click**. As soon as he was inside, the automatic **LIGHTING SYSTEM** turned on and flooded the room with light. All around him were **precious** objects in glass cases.

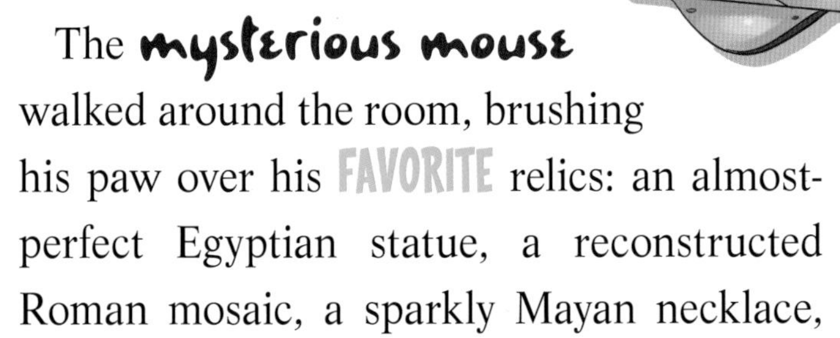

The **mysterious mouse** walked around the room, brushing his paw over his **FAVORITE** relics: an almost-perfect Egyptian statue, a reconstructed Roman mosaic, a sparkly Mayan necklace,

and a medieval crown. Then he approached the back of the room, where the light was fainter and SEVEN EMPTY CASES sparkled in the shadows.

"I will find them, Aurora," he muttered under his breath through clenched teeth. "I will find them all!"

At that moment, the communicator on his wrist **vibrated**.

"Yes, Cassidy," he replied as he **activated** the device.

"We're in France," Cassidy squeaked. "We found the mice. **THERE ARE FIVE OF THEM**."

"Well, who are they? Police? Agents from

some kind of organization? Fanatical archaeologists?"

"No," Cassidy replied. "They are five **students** from Mouseford Academy on Whale Island. They spent their vacation on a farm in Scotland. They're just mouselets . . ."

"What do you mean, they're '**JUST MOUSELETS**'?" the mouse in the bunker thundered. "Then why did they help the old mouse with the tapestry?"

"It seems they did it out of friendship, sir," Cassidy replied.

He responded with a high-pitched cackle. "Friendship?! **The pure spirit of friendship doesn't exist in this world!** They must be five schemers who want to possess the treasures."

"Well, whatever it is they're after, we made an interesting discovery," Cassidy continued.

"It seems the students found Aurora Beatrix Lane's journal."

"A journal?" the mouse replied. "Well, what are you waiting for? Go get it!"

"Well, sir, it's complicated," Cassidy replied. "You see, at the moment, the five mice are on an ISLAND with a former lighthouse keeper named John —"

"I don't care about the details!" the mouse in the bunker shouted, cutting her off. "Just get that journal in whatever way necessary and BRING IT HERE TO ME."

"Understood, sir," Cassidy replied quickly. "I'm on it."

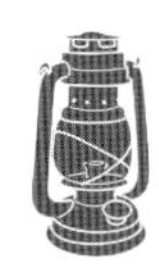

A NASTY SURPRISE

The Thea Sisters thanked John for his invaluable help and promised to let him know what happened during their search.

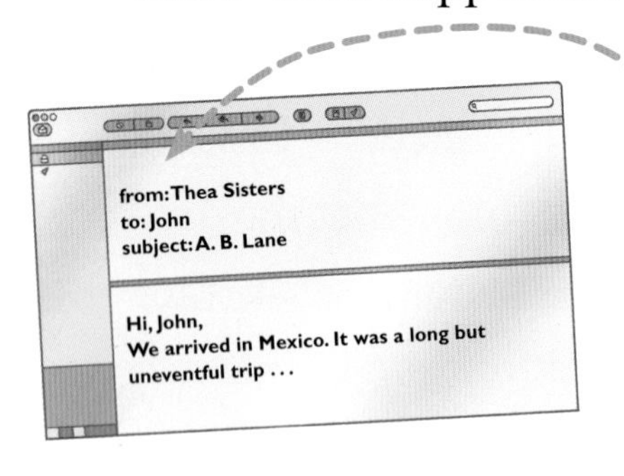

"If you give us your **email** address . . ." Paulina began, but John cut her off.

"**Email?**" He chuckled.

"I don't use these modern inventions."

"Okay, your **telephone number** is fine," Nicky tried.

"I don't have one of those, either!" John laughed.

Colette giggled.

"I understand," she said. "We'll write you a *letter*!"

"Great idea!" he replied happily. "And now, take this."

He gave them a package.

"But that's your notebook with all your **research** about Aurora and her life!" Paulina exclaimed in disbelief.

John nodded. "It's everything that has to do with her **EXPEDITION** in Mexico, the only one I have any information about," he confirmed. "I hope it will be useful to you on your journey."

The Thea Sisters

thanked him again for his help and continued on their mission.

The trip from France to Mexico would be a long one. First, they had to go back to Paris by train, and then take an airplane from there. They were walking along the road that led back to the port when three mice popped out of nowhere.

"Get their backpacks!" a voice cried.

Everything happened in a flash: The mouse in the black hat and sunglasses whom they had SEEN at Beitris's house was there along with the two other suspicious mice.

In no time, they were wrestling with the Thea Sisters as they tried to GRAB their backpacks.

"Come on, let go!" one of the mice cried as he PULLED AT Nicky's backpack.

"I'll help you!" his accomplice said

after he examined and tossed Violet's backpack aside. In a flash, he had grabbed Nicky so the other mouse could take her backpack.

"**HERE IT IS!**" he exclaimed, waving Aurora's diary in the air. "I got it!"

"Give it back!" Colette cried.

The other mouse looked at her mockingly. "What are you going to do about it?"

"I'm going to do THIS!" Colette replied, stomping on the thug's paw. He immediately let go of the journal, and it FLEW out of his paws and spun in the air. Nicky darted forward to GRAB IT, but the other thug was faster.

"Enough games," he THUNDERED THREATENINGLY as he tucked the journal under his jacket.

"Come on!" the mouse in the hat

squeaked. "We got what we came for. **Now let's get out of here!**"

The Thea Sisters grabbed their backpacks and FOLLOWED them as they headed for the port.

"Come on, mouselets!" Pam shouted encouragingly. "We can't let them GET AWAY!"

"There they are!" Paulina exclaimed in dismay, pointing at the three thugs as they boarded a little boat. In a few moments, they would be gone.

"Let's get on this one!" Nicky cried, boarding another small boat docked nearby. Her friends quickly climbed in. Paulina and Nicky began to row vigorously.

Thanks to Nicky's rowing skills, the Thea Sisters were **alongside** the other boat in no time at all.

Violet, who was at the bow, reached out,

Grab the oar!

See ya!
I've got it!

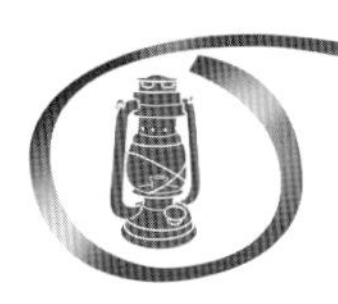

trying to grab the jacket of the mouse with the journal.

"You can do it, Vi!" Colette urged.

Suddenly, the mouse grabbed Violet's arm and pulled her into the water with a splash!

"Violet!" Colette yelled.

Nicky immediately REACHED OUT of the boat to help her as Pam took the oar and brought it near Violet.

"Grab the oar!" Pam yelled.

Luckily, Violet knew how to swim quite well, and with the help of her friends, she was back on the boat in no time.

"Those RATS!" Colette exclaimed, her voice shaking in frustration.

"They're gone," Violet said in disbelief as she wrung out her wet hair. "And they have the journal."

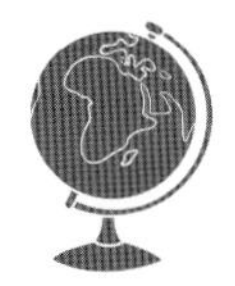

THE NEXT STOP

The Thea Sisters returned to the port, disappointed. Violet had begun to sneeze, so they sought refuge in an inn where she could drink some hot tea and change her clothes.

"I can't stop thinking about Aurora's journal in the paws of those rats," she said, discouraged. "If I had been FASTER, I could have gotten it back."

"Don't blame yourself, Vi!" Colette said. "Those rats were **BIG**, **MEAN**, and very ***determined***. They didn't even hesitate to throw you in the water!"

"Yes, but . . ." Violet cut in.

"The **important** thing is that you're okay,"

Nicky said gratefully. "I just wonder how they knew we had the journal."

"The **restaurant**!" Pam exclaimed suddenly. "Vi, remember that you felt like you were being watched? Those rats probably **FOLLOWED** us and heard us talking about the

journal with Colette's parents!"

Colette opened her mouth in shock. "I wonder who they could be." she said.

"We'll find out soon enough," Paulina continued with a fierce look of DETERMINATION. "But what matters now is that we move FORWARD with our investigation."

"Right!" Colette smiled. "So, what do we know about Aurora's trip to Mexico?"

Pam pulled out John's NOTEBOOK and put it on the table.

"We're lucky they didn't take this!" she said as she opened the book and analyzed its contents. There were old newspaper articles, photos, and notes.

"Ugh, John has TERRIBLE pawwriting!" Pam remarked.

"It's true, but these notes are helpful," Colette replied as she leaned over to take a

MEXICO

Mexico offers tropical jungles, deserts, volcanoes, and fascinating historic cities all in one country. Thanks to the numerous archaeological sites, visiting Mexico is like taking an incredible journey back in time in search of ancient civilizations and treasures of great artistic and cultural worth.

look. "He **reconstructed** Aurora's entire itinerary here. She left England and arrived in Mérida, Yucatán, after various stops. From there she reached the archaeological sites of the **Puuc Route**."

"If the **Yucatán** was her destination, then the treasure could be there," Nicky observed.

"But something doesn't fit," Violet reflected carefully.

"If the treasure was so precious that it needed to be kept a secret, and Aurora intentionally left the tapestry to her sisters as a clue to its location, it's strange that it would be at a famouse site that Aurora visited during the only trip she made public," Violet explained.

Paulina agreed. "It's not likely that we will find the treasure there, but maybe we will find another clue . . . or something else entirely!" Paulina said.

"We should GET MOVING!" Violet declared, putting on her jacket. "This time no one is getting in our way!"

ANOTHER DISAPPOINTMENT

Back in the secret underground laboratory in Alaska, the external communication monitor lit up and an image appeared. It was a worn, old journal.

"That's **Aurora's journal**?" the mysterious mouse asked.

The frame changed and Cassidy's face appeared.

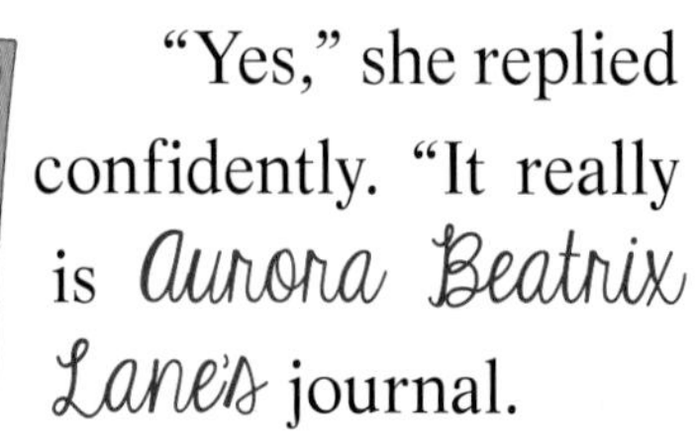

"Yes," she replied confidently. "It really is *Aurora Beatrix Lane's* journal.

"It's nearly a century old, and it

begins on the day she graduated from GIRTON COLLEGE. It tells of her first year as an archaeologist, and of how her —"

"Enough!" the mouse in the laboratory squeaked, cutting her off. "What does it say about the treasures? Does it **MENTION** them? Does it *describe* them?"

"Well, she writes about finding the book that contained some sort of ancient legend," Cassidy explained. "And —"

"And it says where to find the treasure, right?" the mouse in Alaska squeaked excitedly, cutting off Cassidy a second time.

"Unfortunately, no," she replied, annoyed. "If you'd let me finish, I would have explained that the journal stops before it gets into any details. It doesn't say anything about the treasure. It only mentions something called the ALABASTER GARDEN."

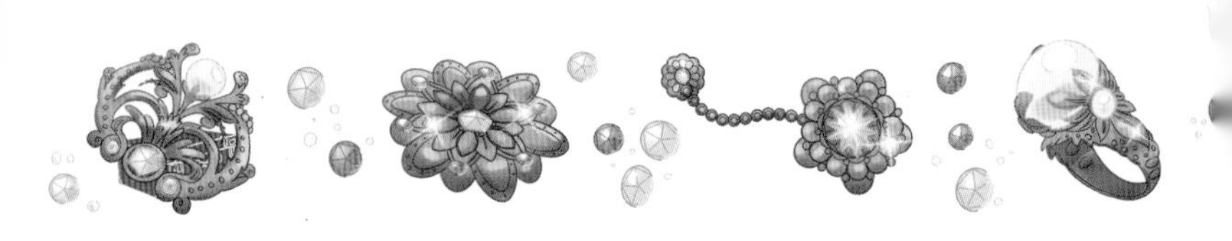

"What?!" the mouse in the lab cried, pounding his paws on his desk in frustration. "That's not possible. It really doesn't reveal the treasure's location?"

"I'm afraid not," Cassidy said.

The mouse was silent for a moment. "Maybe you missed something. Send me a scanned copy," he ordered at last.

"Of course, sir," Cassidy replied.

A moment later all the digitized pages of Aurora's journal appeared on another SCREEN in the laboratory.

The mouse in the underground bunker had abruptly cut off his conversation with Cassidy, and he was now concentrating on the journal. He read each page very carefully,

but just as his assistant had said, there was no specific information about the treasures or where they could be found.

"An ALABASTER GARDEN . . ." he read aloud.

That phrase appeared on the tapestry as well, but it didn't seem familiar to him. It didn't MATCH up with any of the ancient civilizations he knew of.

What could it be about? With his understanding of ancient civilizations, the mouse figured the treasure was probably precious jewels. But where were they hidden?

His frustration growing, he finally reached the last pages of the journal.

12th of February

Dear Diary,

I have almost figured out the location where the first of the seven treasures — the alabaster garden — is hidden. The legend links it to the jewel of the palace.

I'm just missing one small piece of the puzzle.

I'm excited by the idea of bringing that marvel to light, but I'm not sure how to do it. So far I've only shared my research with Robert, and he's warned me often that I have to be very careful. We both realize that a relic of that worth will tempt many mice. So my research will remain a secret for now, especially from Professor von Klawitz.

But once I've found the treasure, will I have to break my silence? Or is there some way to continue to keep the treasure hidden and safe?

Maybe it would be better to find out where the treasure is and then leave the information to a trustworthy mouse.

When I started studying archaeology I never thought I would find myself in such a difficult situation, but as Robert always says:

when you're passionate about something, you have to give it your all.

Dear Robert – I can't wait to hug him again. He has often sent me letters that have been of great comfort.

Take care of yourself, my dearest Aurora. You know that you can always count on me if you ever have a problem.

Robert

Today I went back to Cambridge to say farewell to my teachers.

I'm so filled with emotion from returning to the places where I studied to be an archaeologist.

And now, I think I will leave you here, faithful diary, in a little hiding place I've made.

You will be safe here and I can come to visit you if I ever need to.

Good-bye, my dear diary . . .

The mouse shook his head in irritation.

"As usual, *aurora* just provides more questions than answers," he grumbled. Then he called Cassidy back.

"This diary is **useless**," he growled, annoyed. "What happened to the five mice?"

"They're **TRAVELING** again," came Cassidy's reply.

"Really?" the mouse replied. "How very interesting. Start **following** them again. I have a feeling they will lead us to something this time."

MEXICO, HERE WE COME!

The Thea Sisters arrived in Mérida, Mexico, on a Saturday afternoon. They found it to be a BRIGHT and **vivacious** city, dotted with lush green palm trees and rich with elegant buildings and monuments.

"It would be marvemouse to have time to see the city," Colette said with a sad sigh.

"It's true, but our mission is more important," Nicky replied. "Let's get started!"

"But how do we do that?" Violet wondered aloud.

"Let's sit down somewhere and go through John's pages so we can decide what to do next." Paulina suggested.

"Sounds good to me!" Pam exclaimed.

What a beautiful city!
And what amazing food . . .

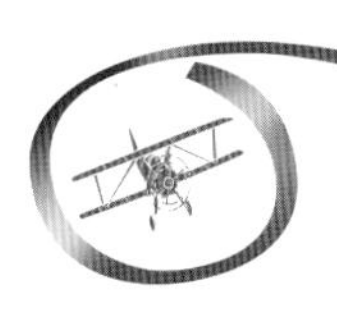

A few minutes later the mouselets were seated around an outdoor table at a local café, where they ordered *papadzules* — tortillas dipped in a pumpkin seed sauce and filled with hard-boiled egg. As they finished their meal with some *dulce de papaya* — papaya served in a syrup and topped with cheese — Paulina took out John's **NOTEBOOK** and began to look through it.

"According to John's notes, Aurora had decided to take the **PUUC ROUTE**, an ancient road south of Mérida that goes past ancient Mayan ruins at Uxmal, Kabah, Sayil, Xlapak, and Labná," Paulina explained.

"So the idea is to follow the Puuc Route and trace Aurora's **TRACKS**, right?" Violet asked.

"Exactly," Paulina replied, nodding. "There's just one problem: According to

THE PUUC ROUTE

From 250–900 CE, in the land we now call Mexico, the classic Maya civilization flourished and grew to around forty cities. The Mayans dedicated themselves to art, architecture, mathematics, and astronomy, and had their own hieroglyphic writing system. Today, many former Mayan cities are among the most famouse archaeological sites in the world. These include the cities along the Yucatán Peninsula's Puuc Route, which connects the cities of Uxmal, Kabah, Sayil, Xlapak, and Labná.

John's research, Aurora visited more than one of the sites."

Violet let out a tired **sigh**. "That means we need to stop at each **SITE**, hoping Aurora left some trace of her journey," she said.

"Or maybe she left some new clues that will lead us to the **treasure**," Colette

added hopefully.

"That's going to take some time," Pam said.

"Is there any one place in particular that John mentions in his notes?" Nicky asked. "Maybe we could start there."

"Unfortunately, no," Paulina replied as she flipped through the pages of the notebook again. "The only thing that's mentioned is the **Puuc Route**."

Then, suddenly, she stopped.

"Wait a minute . . ." Paulina said as she got to the end of the notebook. "This might help!"

"It's a letter from Aurora to Robert!" Paulina exclaimed. "Maybe it has some useful clues!"

"Come on, let's read it!" Violet proposed with a new enthusiasm.

Everyone gathered around Paulina to read.

Mérida, September 8

My dearest Robert,

Mexico is simply marvemouse! It's a lively and beautiful country, and the people are happy and welcoming. Plus, the Yucatán peninsula is extraordinary: There are lush green forests all around me, with ancient pyramids scattered throughout.

Today I began my travels. I'm using this trip to work, but also to reflect. The discovery I made seven months ago still gives me much to think about. Was it wise to keep it hidden?

In the end, I decided to only trust my journal. I already finished it and left it in the depths of an invisible place, guarded by the chattiest of animals.

My dearest friend, even here I miss you.

See you soon.
Yours,
Aurora

"I don't understand," Nicky said, scratching her forehead. "What did she find **seven months earlier**?"

"And the end, where she talks about the invisible place?" Pam commented, a confused look on her snout. "It's INCOMPREHENSIBLE . . ."

But Violet shook her head. "No, I think I've got it," she said slowly. "The finding that she kept hidden could be the first treasure."

Colette nodded. "And she didn't **tell** anyone about it . . ."

"Except the second journal!" Paulina jumped in. "It sounds like she hid it just like the first journal we found at Girton."

"Yes, 'in the depths of an invisible place, guarded by the chattiest of animals . . .'" Nicky repeated the words slowly. "It must be some sort of CODED message to lead Robert to the diary!"

"That's right," Violet agreed with a nod. "We just need to **decipher** the message and find the second journal, which will lead to the **treasure**!"

"Hmm . . . an invisible place," Pam **reflected**. "Maybe it's a place that is so dark that at night it disappears."

"And the chattiest of animals?" Nicky

continued. "I don't even know what kind of **animals** live here in the Yucatán."

Paulina took out her TABLET and began to tap away.

"Ah!" she finally exclaimed. "I figured out where we need to **GO**: to the university library, where we can find information about the local area. I'm sure we will find something there that's **useful**!"

A NEW FRIEND

The library was located in a big palace in the center of the city. There, the Thea Sisters immediately got some books about geography and local traditions. Finding the right information regarding Aurora's RIDDLE wasn't so easy, though.

"Have you FOUND anything?" Pam asked Colette, who was seated near her, behind a pile of enormouse bound volumes.

"Not yet," her friend replied. "I've read through volume after volume, but it seems like an impossible task!"

An elderly mouse wearing thick glasses cleared his throat loudly. He seemed annoyed by their chatter.

"I know," Pam said. "I don't know where else to look!"

"If you want to try an encyclopedia, please help yourself!" Colette proposed.

"Shhh!" the irritated mouse hissed loudly.

"I'm sorry," Colette muttered. Then she turned toward her friend, lowering her voice. "The INVISIBLE PLACE isn't mentioned anywhere. We don't even know if it's a town or a place in the jungle!"

"Come on, now!" the grumpy old mouse squeaked again.

Colette's fur turned bright red, and she lowered her snout into her ENCYCLOPEDIA. She had just begun reading again when something landed on the desk next to her paw. Stunned, she picked up the object and realized that it was a crumpled piece of paper. She smoothed out the paper and read the following: **UXMAL**

Colette looked around to see where the paper had come from and noticed a young mouse with twinkling eyes and dark whiskers sitting at the desk next to hers.

"I think the invisible place is Uxmal," the mouse whispered to Colette. "The site was **ABANDONED** and covered in thick vegetation, making it practically invisible until the nineteenth century, when archaeologists brought it back to the *light* of day."

The mouse in the **glasses** stood up dramatically and closed his books.

"This is **TOO MUCH**," he huffed loudly. "I am going to complain to the director of the library!"

Colette was mortified, but she didn't think they had been talking **that** loudly.

"Why did you write me that message?"

Colette whispered softly to the young mouse so she wouldn't disturb anyone else.

"Let's go outside," he replied.

Colette signaled to Pam that she would be right back, and then she followed the mouse.

"Hi, I'm Diego," the friendly mouse said, introducing himself. "I heard you squeaking with your friend before about an INVISIBLE place, and I thought that it might be Uxmal."

"I'm Colette," she replied. "That's an archaeological site on the Puuc Route, right?"

"That's right," Diego replied, holding out his paw to her.

Colette couldn't contain her excitement. She grabbed his paw happily.

"That's fantastic!" she squeaked. "You just helped me solve a big puzzle!"

"Great to meet you," Diego replied. "What's this puzzle about?"

"Well, my friends and I are **LOOKING** for someone," Colette explained. "I mean something. An old journal, actually."

"In Uxmal?" Diego asked, a perplexed look on his snout.

Colette nodded. "My **friends** and I have to get there right away. Can you tell me where it is?"

"It's about fifty miles from here," Diego replied. "If you want, I can take you. I know the area **very well**. I'm studying to be a tour guide."

"That sounds great," Colette replied. "But first I'd better find my **friends**."

"Do you mean these four mice?" Diego asked, pointing to Paulina, Pam, Violet, and Nicky as they ***approached***.

"We haven't found anything," Violet said with a sigh. "Did you, Coco?"

"Actually, I think I figured out where we need to **go**, thanks to Diego!" Colette explained, gesturing toward her new friend.

"Nice to meet you all," he said.

"Diego is studying to be a tour guide and he offered to take us to **UXMAL**, the invisible city," Colette explained.

"The invisible city!" Violet exclaimed excitedly. "Of course!"

"Do you have a car?" Diego asked. He glanced at his watch. "Because the last bus for Uxmal left **exactly** five minutes ago."

"Oh no!" Colette groaned. "What bad luck! We don't have a car."

"I have an idea," Diego offered. "Why don't you stay at my family's home tonight as my guests? First thing **TOMORROW MORNING**, I will accompany you to Uxmal."

"Really?" Colette asked tentatively. "But

there are five of us. We don't want to interfere with your **PLANS**."

"It's no problem at all," Diego replied with a smile. "I have no plans tomorrow, and I can practice being a tour guide. You'll just have to **squeeze** together a bit at my house!"

That's how the five friends met Diego's **friendly** parents, grandparents, and his little brothers. Then Diego insisted on showing them around Mérida's main street, the **Paseo de Montejo**.

"Tonight there is a special musical festival featuring traditional songs and dances," Diego explained as he guided the Thea Sisters through the **CROWD**.

For a while, the Thea Sisters were able to put aside thoughts of their investigation and **relax** and **have fun**. Only when it was finally time for **BED** a few hours later did

What a beautiful festival!

Paulina think about their mission again.

"I really hope we find the journal," she whispered to Colette.

"I have a GOOD feeLING about Uxmal," Colette said with a smile.

"Well then, good night," Paulina said with a yawn. "We'd better get some rest. We have a big day ahead of us!"

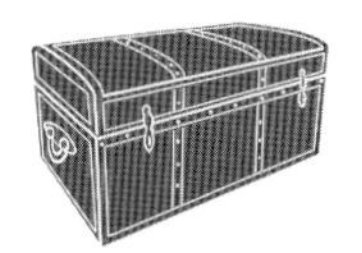

PYRAMIDS IN THE JUNGLE

The next **morning**, Colette felt something — or someone — sitting on top of her sleeping bag. When she opened her eyes, she was snout-to-snout with Gabriel, Diego's **youngest** brother.

"My brother says that it's time for you to **wake up**!" he squeaked.

"Who? What?" Violet said groggily as she sat up and rubbed her eyes. It took her a moment to recall **where** she was and **why**.

Pam jumped out of her sleeping bag. "I smell the **delicious** scent of fried eggs. I don't know about the rest of you, but I'm **HUNGRY**!"

She ***headed*** straight to the kitchen,

where the table was set with eggs, beans, tortillas, and salsa.

Pam had been sitting there for a while when the other Thea Sisters joined her and sat down to breakfast with Diego's family.

"Are you ready to go?" Diego asked, appearing in the doorway. "The bus is supposed to LEAVE soon."

"We're ready!" Colette squeaked. She and her friends thanked Diego's family for their hospitality and gave them a warm good-bye. Then they were off toward **UXMAL**.

"Uxmal is one of the most well-preserved archaeological sites in the Yucatán," Diego began explaining once they were on the bus. "Its name means '**BUILT THREE TIMES**' in ancient Mayan because its tallest building, the Pyramid of the Magician, was built in various stages."

"Wow, you know a lot about this area," Nicky commented. "You're a terrific guide!"

"At your SERVICE!" Diego responded with a wink. "I love to show visitors the wonders of the Yucatán. Ask me anything you want!"

"I have a question . . . when will we get there?!" Violet asked, her snout pale. The rough road was making her feel ILL.

"Don't worry, we're nearly there!" Diego reassured them.

A few minutes later, the bus pulled up to the entrance to the site.

"But we're in the middle of the forest!" Colette said in disbelief.

"That's right," Diego said. "The buildings at Uxmal are surrounded by jungle. Do you want to see them all or are you interested in one particular place?"

Colette quickly explained the RIDDLE and the mention of the chattiest animal.

"Follow me!" Diego said, leading them to the other end of the site. The Thea Sisters couldn't help but admire the well-preserved stone ruins, which rose IMPOSINGLY from the lush green forest that surrounded them.

"What a marvemouse place," Violet whispered in awe as Diego stopped at the foot of a TALL STONE PYRAMID with many stairs.

"Yes, and luckily it doesn't seem like anyone is following us this time," Pam said with a sigh of relief as she took in the groups of harmless-looking tourists around them.

"Let's go up," Diego said as he began to climb the STEEP steps at a brisk pace. The Thea Sisters quickly followed him. Once they arrived at the top, they understood why Diego had taken them there: The top of the pyramid was adorned with carvings of MACAWS.

"Of course!" Violet said. "The CHATTIEST OF ANIMALS . . ."

"This is called the Temple of the Macaws," Diego explained, gesturing to the structure at the top of the pyramid.

Paulina peeked inside. "Maybe what we're looking for is in there," she said.

Colette had told Diego about Aurora's journal, so he understood what she meant.

"Wait!" he said quickly. "Entering the temple is FORBIDDEN."

"But Aurora's journal must be in there!" Paulina exclaimed.

"Thanks for the information!" a tourist near them hissed suddenly.

He had long blond hair and was wearing a flowered shirt, but the Thea Sisters

recognized him as one of the two thugs who had followed them to the Île de Sein: They were in disguise! His accomplice was wearing a pair of glasses and fake whiskers. He quickly slipped inside the temple and came out a short while later with a PACKAGE in his paw.

"They got the journal!" Pam squeaked in dismay.

"They're not going to get away this time!" Nicky cried as she quickly SNATCHED the package that the mouse was holding.

"Run, Nicky, run!" Paulina yelled.

Nicky sprinted down the stairs as quickly as she could while her friends tried to STOP the two thugs. The mouse in the flowered shirt began to run after Nicky. He had almost reached her when Diego suddenly jumped in front of him, blocking his path.

The rat yelled to his accomplice: "Max, you get her!"

But the rat in the glasses and fake whiskers remained frozen at the top of the pyramid.

"I . . . I can't," he squeaked nervously. "I can't go down. It's too high and I'm afraid of heights!"

I'm afraid of heights . . .
Run to the bus!
We're coming!

This way!

"**You're what?!**" the other rat yelled, but by then Diego and the Thea Sisters had already darted down the stairs behind Nicky.

"Go!" Diego called. "I'll stay here and distract them. You get to the bus and get on it!"

"Thank you **SO MUCH**!" Colette said.

Soon the five mouselets emerged from the emerald-green forest in an open clearing. There was a bus there that was about to ***LEAVE*** for Campeche, in the south.

"**LET'S GO!**" Pam cried out.

They boarded the bus quickly and sat down in the back, their **HEARTS** pounding.

Nicky slowly took the diary out of the cloth it was wrapped in. They had done it! **They had found Aurora's second journal!**

THE FINAL RIDDLE

As soon as the bus began to move and they were sure they were safe, the Thea Sisters opened the **journal**.

"It's incredible," Paulina said, in awe at their discovery. "I can't **believe** we managed to *find it*."

"I'm worried about Diego," Colette said anxiously. "I hope they don't do anything to him."

Poor Diego!

"He'll be okay, Coco," Violet reassured her. "They were looking for the journal, and he has **nothing to do with it**. Let's start reading!"

22nd of February

Dear Diary,

All my research has finally paid off. I've found the first of the seven ancient treasures.

It wasn't easy, but I was able to reconstruct the legendary path to the treasure piece by piece. And I was able to find the legendary alabaster garden without being discovered.

In fact, dear Diary, by now it is very clear to me that Professor von Klawitz is looking to get his paws on the treasure.

For that reason, I have made an important decision. I will look for the six other treasures as well. I will find them, and I will stop Klawitz from getting to them by erasing every trace that leads me to each treasure.

I will preserve a key that leads to each treasure. This way if something happens to me, a trusted person will be able to find each one. I will give a key to each of my sisters.

For this first treasure, I will give Petra the tapestry.

She will use it to find the alabaster garden in a place that unites

---

Kenya, Argentina, Nepal, Nicaragua, Australia, Uruguay, and Robert's nephew.

"Another riddle!" Nicky chuckled. "I've **grown fond** of Aurora's puzzles."

"Let's try to solve this one quickly . . . I feel like we're so close to solving this mystery!"

POTENTIAL SOLUTIONS TO THE RIDDLE:

1. Do the countries that are named BORDER the treasure's location?

2. Is there a place that has SOMETHING IN COMMON with all these countries?

3. Does Robert's nephew HAVE A CONNECTION to these countries?

4. Does something else about these countries connect them, like a COLOR or a NUMBER?

5. Do the INITIALS of the countries and of John's name make up the name of a place?

ANSWERS

1. The countries are in different parts of the world, so this is impossible.
2. That seems unlikely.
3. Probably not: John was still young and hadn't left England yet.
4. Not really.
5. Yes! This must be the answer!

"K-A-N-N-A-U-J," Colette said slowly. "Could that be right? Is that a real place? And where is it?"

Paulina quickly consulted her tablet.

"It **IS** a real place!" she replied. "And it's in India! It's in Uttar Pradesh, in the northern part of the country."

Pam clapped her paws in excitement.

"Holey cheese, sisters!" she squeaked "We **really** found the location of the treasure!"

FIVE MICE TOO MANY

Meanwhile, back in his underground lair, the **mysterious** mouse in Alaska was furious.

"How is that possible?" he squeaked angrily at the screen, where the faces of his henchmice Max and Stan appeared. He knew from the **LOOKS** on their **snouts** that they hadn't succeeded in their mission.

"We had the journal in our paws, but those **CLEVER MOUSELETS** managed to grab it and run off!" Stan replied.

"And they had an **accomplice** this time," Max added. "He **got in the way** and misled us!"

"Were you at least able to capture him and question him?" the mouse in the lab asked.

Max and Stan were silent for a moment

as they recalled the scene: They had followed Diego, but he jumped on the bus to Mérida and waved at them as it pulled away, amused.

"Um, n-no actually —" Stan stuttered.

"Forget it," the mouse in the bunker replied, cutting him off. "I should fire you and hire mice who can actually do their jobs. But there's no time: I must find Aurora's treasure before those **FIVE MICE** do!"

"But they have the **journal**," Stan muttered.

"Yes, and the journal **must be recovered**," his boss replied. "But this time, I'll do it **myself**."

He ended the conversation and began punching in some commands on his keyboard. A second monitor LIT UP, and information from a database began to

FLASH across the screen. The mouse's eyes darted from one image to the next until the system stopped on a screen with several small squares. Five of them lit up.

"Colette. Pamela. Violet. Nicky. Paulina," the mouse read the names aloud. "What do you all have to do with *Aurora*?"

A moment later, a description of the Thea Sisters' vacation in Scotland appeared.

"Could this all be a **coincidence**?" the mouse wondered. "I didn't think it possible, but maybe these students from Mouseford

really are only **interested** in Aurora Beatrix Lane because they want to help this old Scottish mouse."

He pondered the situation for a moment and then began to cackle.

"Well, whatever their MOTIVATION, those students haven't **beaten** me yet," he squeaked confidently. "They still don't know **WHO** they're dealing with . . ."

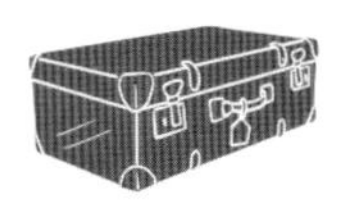

THE SCENT OF INDIA

The Thea Sisters were hot and tired when they reached Campeche after the long bus ride.

Even though they couldn't wait to leave for India, they knew it would be wiser to STOP for a night, get some rest, and maybe do some laundry before leaving.

"Paulina, will you handle planning the trip?" Pam asked her friend once they were settled in at their hotel.

"Yes, but I'll have to be very careful," Paulina replied. "Those thugs have managed to follow us everywhere. I don't want any SURPRISES this time."

Colette holding Aurora's journal.

"You're right," she agreed. "We're just one step from the treasure. I know we can do it!"

Paulina sat down at the computer in the hotel where they were staying and began planning their trip to India. They would land in Lucknow, a large city in Uttar Pradesh with the airport closest to Kannauj. Paulina purposefully added extra layovers to their itinerary to mislead anyone who might try following them on their journey.

KANNAUJ

The city of Kannauj is in northern India, in the region of Uttar Pradesh close to the Ganges River. This ancient city is known as a center for the distillation and production of tobacco, perfume, and rose water.

Violet, Pamela, Colette, and Nicky sat next to Paulina around the computer. Violet had read and reread the section in her **GUIDEBOOK** that talked about where they were going.

"This is interesting," she said as she looked up from her book. "Kannauj is known as the city of perfumes. Does that mean anything to you?"

"Hmm," Colette said as she thought hard. "Wait . . . didn't the tapestry mention a place where 'sweet winds blow'? Maybe it means a place where the air is full of fragrances!"

Violet nodded in agreement. "I think you're right, Coco," she said. "I really do think that Aurora's riddle is pointing to Kannauj. She probably had the tapestry made here in India, sprinkling it with clues that we're only just now able to decipher."

"Well, the parts about petals, dawn,

midnight, the friend, and the palace jewel are still mysteries to me!" Nicky said, disheartened.

But Pam was optimistic. "Even if we don't have ALL the answers yet, we're almost there!" she squeaked hopefully. "We will find the ALABASTER GARDEN, I can feel it! Now let's all go to bed and get some rest."

The next morning the friends woke up early and headed to the airport.

"Good-bye, Mexico," Colette said as she looked at the landscape below her while the plane rose into the sky over Campeche. "What a beautiful country."

"Have you heard anything from Diego?" Pam asked.

Colette nodded. "He left me a video message to let me know he was okay."

"Oh, good!" Pam squeaked, relieved. "He

really helped us a lot."

Violet and Paulina spent the flight **organizing** their next few stops. Before landing in Lucknow, they would make **three stopovers** in other countries. When they finally reached India, the group planned to head **immediately** to Kannauj.

As soon as they stepped off the plane in **India**, the five friends were inundated with an intoxicating mix of **smells** and **colors**.

"What a beautiful city," Nicky commented as she **LOOKED** around.

"Lucknow is the capital of Uttar Pradesh," Violet informed them. "It's a city that's rich in palaces and gardens."

"*And where are we going?*" Colette asked.

"Straight to the train station," Paulina replied. "We need to get to Kannauj quickly."

I'll tell you about Kannauj . . .
Here we go!

A short while later, they were standing in front of an imposing white-and-red station next to an enormouse park full of lush GREEN GRASS.

Once they were on the train, the friends went over what they were going to do once they arrived.

"We DON'T KNOW where we need to look in Kannauj, right?" Colette asked.

"Actually, we have one CLUE," Nicky replied. "In her journal, Aurora talks about a place with two lakes . . ."

"It's the bird sanctuary!" Violet exclaimed. "I read all about it. The place is called Lakh Bahosi, and there are two shallow lakes that create a natural habitat for many different birds!"

"Nice work, Violet," Paulina said. "Now we know exactly where to go once we arrive."

A few minutes later, the **TRAIN** clattered and slowed, preparing to enter the station.

They had finally reached the city of Kannauj.

IN THE CITY OF PERFUMES

As soon as they stepped out of the train station, the Thea Sisters were surrounded by a COLORFUL, clamorous crowd of mice.

Pam's stomach was grumbling after the long ride.

"I know we have to get to our next destination as soon as possible, but what do you say we stop and have a bite to eat first?" she asked.

"That's a good idea," Violet agreed. "The guidebook notes that there aren't any **restaurants** or AMENITIES at the bird sanctuary. Since we don't know how long we'll be there, it would be a good idea for us to eat something now."

The Thea Sisters picked a **restaurant** near the train station that looked promising. As soon as they were seated, Pam began to study the menu.

"Umm, well, let's see . . ." she said, scratching her head.

"Can't figure it out, Pam?" Nicky teased. "But I was sure you were an EXPERT on food all over the world!"

"I know some of the dishes, but I really can't figure out what some of the others could be," Pam admitted. "For example, what is palak paneer?"

"It's a delicious dish made of cheese cubes cooked in a spinach curry," said a **kind** voice. It was coming from a mouse wearing a traditional blue *shalwar kameez*, which is an outfit that consists of a long shirt and matching pants.

"Thank you!" Colette said. "Would you mind lending us a PAW with the ordering?"

"I would be happy to!" she replied with a smile. "My name is Aditi, and I help out here in my parents' restaurant."

The Thea Sisters quickly introduced themselves as well.

"Let's see, I would recommend the palak paneer," Aditi said. "You should also order some samosas, which are fried dumplings stuffed with vegetables. And for dessert be sure to get some *gulab jamun.* They're delicious doughnut holes made with cardamom and served in a sweet rose syrup."

"**That all sounds fantastic!**" Pam exclaimed.

Once they had placed their order, the Thea Sisters began chatting with Aditi.

"Is this your first time here in Kannauj?" Aditi asked them.

"Yes," Violet replied.

"It's lovely so far," Paulina added.

"Well, you absolutely must visit the **perfume market**!" Aditi said. "Kannauj is FAMOUSE for its perfume production. It is an ancient tradition: For centuries, the essential oil attar, which is made from rose petals, has been made here."

"I would **love** to visit the market. It sounds amazing!" Colette said.

"I go there often," Aditi replied. "If you'd like, I can take you today."

The Thea Sisters exchanged glances.

"That would be nice, but we're here for another reason," Nicky explained. "We need to **get to** the bird sanctuary. We're looking for something precious there."

"Oh, of course," Aditi said kindly. "I understand. Do you know HOW to get there?"

"As a matter of fact, we don't," Paulina said. "Do you have any TIPS?"

"How do you feel about biking?" Aditi replied. "We have a lot of them, and we can lend you five. I would be happy to take you."

"Weren't you going to the market TODAY?"

Aditi smiled sweetly. "It's okay," she said. "I can go tomorrow. But you need me now."

"Thank you!" Paulina said gratefully.

"Sisters, isn't it **amazing** how nice everyone we've met on this trip has been?"

Violet pointed out. "We've met so many new friends who have offered to help us and have asked for nothing in exchange."

"THAT'S TRUE!" Colette agreed.

"Of course, there are also those who have been trying to steal from us," Paulina pointed out. "Though we've met a lot more helpful friends than enemies!"

Aditi returned with a bike for each of the mouselets. It was a ***long ride***, but finally the five friends reached the BIRD SANCTUARY.

They thanked Aditi and said **good-bye** in front of an archway at the sanctuary **ENTRANCE**.

"I wish you the **best of luck** on your search," she said as she **hugged** each of the Thea Sisters before she rode home.

"Now we just have to search the area,

hoping that *Aurora* left some more clues!" Violet said optimistically as they entered the bird sanctuary.

Riding Toward Treasure

The landscape inside the sanctuary was marvemouse: Birds of every size and color flew around the two lakes.

"If we had the tapestry, maybe it would give us a clue to the treasure," Violet said.

"True, but we've managed to figure things out up to now," Paulina pointed out. "Come on, sisters. We can do it this time, too!"

"Why don't we begin looking along the lakeshore?" Nicky suggested.

So they divided into two groups, and each group headed toward one of the two lakes. They searched the shore foot by foot, looking for some clue that would indicate the presence of a treasure.

We'll go this way!

See you soon!

Meanwhile, a
few miles away,
a loud rumble
and a strong wind
caused a small flock
of birds to lift off and
take flight, disappearing
on the horizon.

The noise got **LOUDER** and **LOUDER**, and soon a giant **helicopter** landed in a clearing. The door to the helicopter burst open, and the mouse from Alaska stepped out. He was wearing an elegant overcoat and **MIRRORED** sunglasses that hid his eyes.

A moment later, a small truck burst out of the nearby **SHRUBS**, and Cassidy, Stan, and Max stepped out.

"Sir, our five targets can be found about a MILE from here," Cassidy said.

"I know," he responded, signaling to his pilot as the helicopter took off. Without another word, the mysterious mouse headed toward the BIRD SANCTUARY. His three henchmice followed quickly behind him.

"This time, I promise we'll get the journal, sir," Stan began.

"We'll have it in no time, I guarantee it!" Max added.

"And we won't let those mice ESCAPE again, either, sir!" Cassidy said.

The boss stopped for a moment. Max and Stan had to stop short so they didn't trip over their own paws.

"You haven't understood a single thing, as usual," he said calmly. "I don't care about the journal or about the five mouselets from

Mouseford anymore. They've led us to the **treasure** already. Did you bring the **tapestry**?"

"Of course!" Cassidy replied, **insulted** that he would ask such a simple question.

Their boss waited, tapping his paw.

"Well, where is it?" he finally thundered.

"**Pull it out!**" Cassidy ordered the other two mice.

"You had it!" Max squeaked at Stan.

"No, you did!" Stan replied. "You were supposed to take it."

Cassidy looked up at the sky

and huffed: "I'll get it!"

Then she went back to the truck, her HEELS slipping as they dug into the soft ground.

"Go help her," their boss squeaked impatiently. "Meet up with me when you have it."

Then he strode toward the two lakes as Max and Stan DARTED after Cassidy.

THE PLOT THICKENS!

Meanwhile, the Thea Sisters had finished **EXAMINING** the area and had returned to their starting point.

"**Did anyone find anything?**" Paulina asked her friends.

Nicky shook her head. "I haven't seen anything related to *aurora* or the treasure."

"I wonder if there's someone here we can ask for **information**," Violet pondered.

"Hey, wait a second," Pam said suddenly. "Where's Colette?"

"She was just here a minute ago," Nicky said.

"*Did she get lost?*" Violet asked, worried.

"No, there she is!" Pam exclaimed, pointing

to a **SILHOUETTE** on the horizon. Colette approached them, pedaling quickly. She stopped right in front of her friends, breathless.

"I SAW THEM!" she gasped. "I SAW THEM!"

"Who?" her friends asked.

"The three mice who keep following us!" Colette replied in one breath.

"What?!" Nicky gasped in disbelief. "They followed us all the way here?"

Colette nodded. "Yes, and they're heading **this way**!" she said. "I took a picture on my phone. Look — they're bringing something bulky with them."

They're coming!

Colette showed them her **phone**.

"Wait a minute," Paulina said. "**Zoom** in on this part!"

She tapped the screen, and Colette zoomed in. Violet leaned in to look, too.

"But it can't be," she squeaked. "It's Beitris's **tapestry**!"

The Thea Sisters exchanged glances. They had to move **quickly** if they were going to outwit the three thugs.

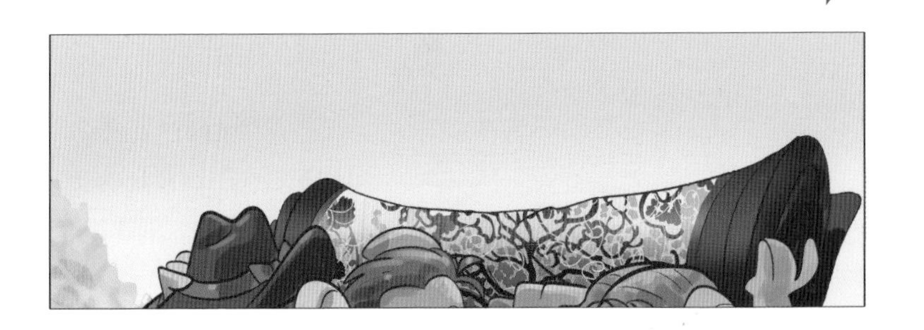

"I say this time we need to do the **opposite** of what we usually do," Pam suggested.

"Exactly!" Nicky agreed. "We should be the ones to **SURPRISE** them!"

"Two of us could distract them, and the others could sneak up behind them," Violet said. "They don't know we're coming, so we'll have that to our advantage."

"And it's five against three!" Pam added.

Colette nodded. "Agreed! I'll lead you to them, and Pam and I will **distract them**."

A few moments later, the plan was put into action. Max, Stan, and Cassidy weren't moving quickly. Stan and Max were **WEIGHED DOWN** by the bulky, rolled-up tapestry, and Cassidy's high heels kept getting stuck in the soft ground.

Once the three thugs came into **VIEW**, Pam and Colette approached them quickly and stopped right in front of them, **BLOCKING** their path.

As soon as Max and Stan saw Pam and Colette, they reacted.

"**LET'S GET THEM!**" they yelled.

"No, stop!" Cassidy wailed. "The boss isn't interested in them!"

But it was too late: Her accomplices dashed toward the Thea Sisters. Pam took advantage of the fact that the two mice were **burdened** by the tapestry. She stuck out her paw and made Stan trip, causing him to drop the tapestry.

At the same time, Nicky and Paulina snuck up behind Max and caught him by surprise. He tripped over Stan, and the two mice and the tapestry were soon tangled up on the ground.

"What are you two doing?" Cassidy

squeaked furiously. "Do I have to do everything myself?"

She dashed toward the tapestry and scooped it up, but as soon as she had it, she SLIPPED on the muddy ground. Violet was right there, ready to grab the tapestry out of Cassidy's paws.

"It's better to wear comfortable shoes on adventures like this one!" Colette cried with a chuckle as she, Paulina, Pamela, and Nicky sprinted after Violet.

The Thea Sisters headed for their bikes as quickly as possible.

Ouch!
Get back here!
Run, Violet!

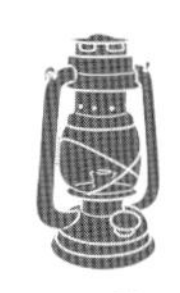

FOLLOWING THE PETALS

Once they hopped on the bikes, the five friends pedaled hard, their **hearts** pounding in their chests. Nicky balanced the heavy tapestry on her handlebars, being careful not to fall.

"**Look over there!**" Colette squeaked, pointing to an abandoned building just outside the sanctuary. The friends stashed their bikes behind the building and hurried inside. It was clear to them that the building must have been beautiful and well-kept at one time, though it showed signs of wear and **disrepair**.

"I think this is where people who took care of the irrigation canals worked," Paulina said. "It's a big public office that's been **abandoned**."

"Well, it's the safest place we have available to us at the moment," Nicky said as she carefully unrolled the tapestry.

Colette read the woven text around the tree once more:

"In the land where sweet winds blow,
Follow the petals: What lies below?
Remember: Midnight comes along
before the sun rises amid birdsong.
There you will find a priceless delight,
An alabaster garden, true and bright.
Created by one who was dear and true
to the jewel of the palace, like me to you.
The guard is a friend with feet so deep,
In its arms this precious gift will keep."

"We know now that the **first line** refers to Kannauj," Colette said. "But what about the **REST** of the poem?

"There doesn't seem to be anything in the park called the alabaster garden, and there are no palaces with **JEWELS**," Nicky said, confused.

Suddenly, Violet hit her paw to her forehead. "Why didn't

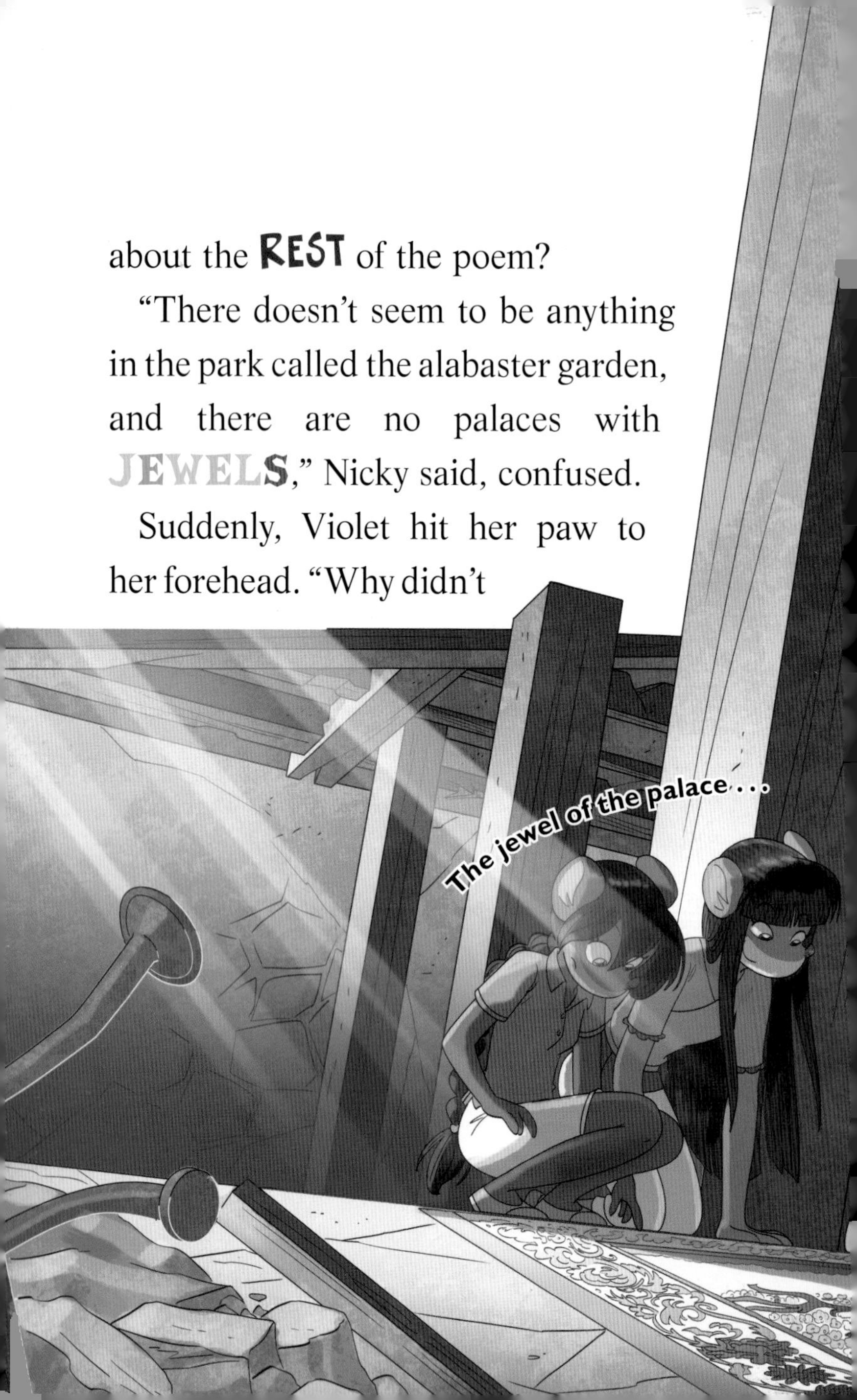

I think of it!" she squeaked. "The jewel of the palace **isn't actually a jewel**!"

"What do you mean, Vi?" Colette asked.

"We are in Uttar Pradesh, India," Violet explained. "The most important monument here is the **Taj Mahal**, which the emperor had built in memory of his wife . . ."

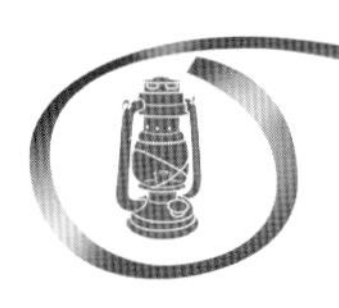

"Are you trying to give us a history lesson?" Pam interrupted.

Violet ignored her friend and continued: "The emperor loved his wife, the princess **Arjumand Banu Begum**, so much that he gave her the nickname Mumtaz Mahal, which means 'jewel of the palace'!"

"Do you mean that Aurora found a treasure that belonged to an ancient princess?!" Nicky exclaimed.

"No, it sounds like the treasure belonged to someone who loved the princess," Violet said. "The tapestry reads 'one who was dear and true to the jewel of the palace.' So maybe it was a sister or a friend!"

"What a beautiful story," Colette said. She passed her paw over the tapestry, admiring the flowers that decorated it. Suddenly, she noticed something she hadn't realized before.

"How strange," she said. "The petals on these flowers seem to be **raised**."

Paulina leaned over to take a look.

"You're right, Coco!" she exclaimed. "These petals haven't been **WOVEN** — they were **applied** to the tapestry later."

"'Follow the petals: What lies below . . .'" Violet repeated. "Coco, do you have that manicure set your mother gave you?"

"Huh?" Colette asked, confused. But she pulled a **small pouch** out of her back pocket. "Yes, of course. Here it is."

Colette handed the set to Violet. Then, to the great astonishment of her friends, Violet pulled out the scissors and began to **CUT THE PETALS**.

Colette couldn't hold back a squeak: "What are you doing?!"

"I'm seeing what lies below the petals,"

Violet explained calmly. "And I would say it has something to do with numbers!"

The friends looked down at the petals Violet had removed. They had revealed a numerical sequence embroidered on the tapestry below.

"Amazing!" Nicky whispered in awe.

"But we're back at **SQUARE ONE**!" Pam exclaimed, frustrated. "How will we ever figure out what these numbers mean?"

But Nicky just smiled. "Don't worry, Pam,"

she squeaked happily. "For once, one of Aurora's RIDDLES is perfectly clear to me! When you have to point to a location in GEOMETRY, what do you use?"

"COORDINATES!" Paulina exclaimed. "They're coordinates! And midnight comes before day, so the numbers on the first flower refer to the north, which is also called midnight."

"Yes, exactly," Nicky confirmed. "And the numbers on the second flower refer to the east, where the sun rises. So the northern latitude is 26 degrees, 55 minutes, and 24.638 seconds, and the eastern longitude is 79 degrees, 37 minutes, and 17.566 seconds!"

"I didn't understand a thing you just said, but YOU ROCK!" Pam cried, throwing her arms around Nicky's neck.

Meanwhile, Paulina was already inserting

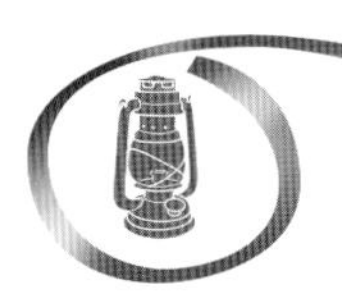

the coordinates into the GPS application on her phone to determine the exact location.

"Here it is," Paulina said. "It's a point right at the center of the BIRD SANCTUARY. We should head back there right away."

"Yes, but we'll need to be careful," Colette warned. "Remember that those thugs are still out there!"

TRAPPED!

The Thea Sisters got back on their bikes. Nicky balanced the **tapestry** on her handlebars again as the five friends pedaled cautiously, keeping a sharp eye out for Cassidy, Stan, and Max.

"There they are!" Pamela shouted, pointing in the distance. "Down there! They're heading this way. Quick, **let's hide**!"

A moment later, the Thea Sisters and their bikes were covered by the bushes. Stan and Max passed nearby without noticing them.

"We're going to be in trouble this time," Max complained.

"We let those **MICE** get the better of us again!" Stan agreed, shaking his snout.

The Thea Sisters held their breath as the two mice hurried by, **grumbling** and **complaining**.

When they had finally passed, the Thea Sisters stepped out of their **HIDING** place.

"Back on the bikes, sisters!" Paulina urged.

A few minutes later, the friends had

reached the location of the coordinates.

They were expecting to find a CAVE or some sort of remote clearing that housed a sparkling garden created by a dear friend of Mumtaz Mahal. But all the Thea Sisters saw in front of them was a field that seemed just like the rest of the BIRD SANCTUARY. The only remarkable thing about the location was a large tree growing from what looked like a cement pedestal.

"Is it possible this is where the treasure is hidden?" Pam asked as she circled the tree.

"Maybe things have changed since Aurora's day, and the treasure doesn't exist anymore," Violet said sadly.

"Well, I think it's here!" Nicky squeaked confidently. "We just need to figure out where it's hiding."

The friends looked around without talking.

But then a high-pitched squeak broke the silence.

"Aha!" the voice said. "I found you!"

The Thea Sisters found themselves snout-to-snout with the **WOMAN** in the black hat and sunglasses who had been following them for days.

"Why are you tracking *Aurora* . . . and **US**?" Nicky asked.

"That doesn't concern you," the mouse replied as she **GRABBED** Pam by the arm. "Tell me where the treasure is."

"You're hurting me!" Pam squeaked.

Nicky was about to run to her friend's defense, but Violet put her paw out to stop her. The Thea Sisters **LOOKED** at one another. There were **FIVE** of them and just one of her. The power of their friendship was **strong** enough to defeat her without

I found you!
Ouch!
You again!

fighting back. Nicky formulated a plan in her mind, and she just needed to look at the others to get their agreement. The others trusted their friend.

"It's here!" Nicky said as she grabbed Pam by the arm, taking a few steps. "This is the place."

"Here?" Cassidy replied, bewildered. "But there's NOTHING here."

Nicky gave Colette a LOOK, and her friend jumped in.

"But it is," Colette squeaked. "It's right here."

Violet suddenly understood Nicky's plan.

"That's right," Violet added. "The treasure isn't buried, it's HIGH UP in those trees!"

Cassidy was so eager to find the treasure that she went ***ahead***, lifting her gaze. She wasn't paying attention to where she was putting her paws, and a second later, she had tumbled down into the **HOLE** that had almost tripped up Paulina earlier. The earth was soft and eased the fall, but the hole was deep enough to keep Cassidy trapped there. Meanwhile, the Thea Sisters raced back to the **enormouse** tree in the clearing.

THE ALABASTER GARDEN

When they reached the clearing, Colette approached the **GIANT** tree.

"You know, Violet," Colette began, "when you told that rat the treasure was in the trees, you made me think of something . . ."

"What do you mean?" Violet asked.

"This could be exactly where the treasure is hidden," Colette explained. "Maybe this tree is the treasure, or maybe . . ."

"Maybe it's the friend who guards it!" Pam exclaimed.

"'The guard is a friend with feet so deep. . .'"

"Yes!" Violet exclaimed, smiling.

"So where is the ALABASTER GARDEN?" Paulina asked, looking around uncertainly.

"The last line on the tapestry is 'In its arms this precious gift will keep,'" Nicky recited. "Let's look at the tree more closely."

The Thea Sisters surrounded the tree and began to examine its THICK trunk.

"'In its arms . . .'" Colette whispered to herself. "Maybe the arms are the branches?"

"Yes, but they're so thick and high," Nicky remarked. "Could they really hold a treasure?"

Suddenly, Paulina gasped.

"Look!" she cried. She pointed to part of the tree's trunk that seemed almost braided

together. Right at her eye level, there was what looked like a WOODEN nest.

In it was a small BOX with the initials ABL carved into the lid.

"It's the treasure," Paulina said. She gently lifted the box from the nest and placed it on the grass as her friends gathered around it. Paulina opened it to find a piece of paper with familiar pawwriting. They picked up the paper and discovered an object underneath.

For a moment, everything around them seemed to get quiet: The songs of numerous birds, the sounds of nearby animals, and even the rustle of the leaves in the trees all STOPPED.

The paper was a letter from Aurora, which the Thea Sisters began to read . . .

There was a small, elegant alabaster vial

Dearest Petra,

Your intrepid and pure soul has led you here. If you have found this box, it means I didn't manage to complete my mission, and I am trusting you with the precious result.

You have the perfume of the earth in your hands. It is the essence that Mumtaz Mahal's handmaid prepared for her with the most precious essences from their garden. It was created with ancient herbs, and there is no purer scent in the world. Despite the fact that it is centuries old, this perfume is so refined that it hasn't evaporated or lost its power. Perhaps this is because it was created by a friend for a friend, and true friendship never dies. It is an incredibly rare artifact, but I think its greatest value is that it reminds us how precious our Earth is and how long-lasting friendship can be. Take care of it, sweet Petra, as I would have done.

Aurora

in the box, and it sparkled like a jewel. The top and the bottle were decorated with the carvings of many different flowers — symbols of strength and fragility.

An inscription in golden letters at the bottom of the vial read: THE PERFUME OF THE EARTH.

"Wouldn't it be so wonderful to open the VIAL and find out what it smells like?" Violet asked.

"Yes, we finally found the ALABASTER GARDEN," Colette agreed. "It isn't a garden after all, but a scent. I'm sure it's the most *beautiful* fragrance in the WORLD."

The Thea Sisters LOOKED at one another, and a feeling of **understanding** passed between them. Though all of them wanted to open the vial to smell the perfume, they knew in their **hearts** that they had to preserve the treasure just as they had found it.

LUCKILY, a very faint sweet scent wafted from the top of the vial, and the five friends closed their eyes and enjoyed the ancient fragrance for a moment. They were immediately surrounded by feelings of peace and harmony. At that moment, they understood the true worth of that small vial: It gives the gifts of SERENITY and **love**!

Now that they had finally recovered the first of the seven treasures, the Thea Sisters knew that they were close to completing their **MISSION**. But first they had to decide where to bring the treasure. They knew they had to entrust it to the right mice so that it would always be **SAFE**.

A BLAST FROM THE PAST

The Thea Sisters quickly hatched a plan. The vial was safe for the moment, but they had to **get back** to the city as soon as possible. They wanted to be sure the treasure stayed in India, where it had been found, and they decided to bring it to the nearest UNIVERSITY. From there, it could be donated to a museum or preserved in the best way possible so it could be admired by everyone.

They hopped on their bikes and had almost left the BIRD SANCTUARY when they heard a gruff voice.

"There you are!"

A moment later, four **SILHOUETTES** appeared on the path in front of the friends.

It was Stan, Max, a muddy Cassidy (pulled out of the hole by her colleagues), and an elegant-looking mouse wearing mirrored sunglasses.

The group blocked the entire path, and the Thea Sisters were forced to break and stop to avoid going off the road.

"Let us pass," Paulina protested.

"No way!" the rat in the SUNGLASSES replied, shaking his head.

"Who are you?" Pam asked.

"Someone who would like to enjoy Aurora's treasure."

"Those are Professor von Klawitz's words," Violet squeaked.

The mouse laughed. "My great-grandfather and I have much in common."

The friends looked at one another, surprised. Just as Aurora had a century

before, they were going snout-to-snout with a greedy, RUTHLESS Klawitz!

"We don't want to keep the treasure!" Paulina protested. "We want to carry out Aurora's dream and give the ancient treasures BACK to the world!"

How naïve . . .

Klawitz burst out laughing again. "Then you five are just as naïve as she was. Now tell me: Where is the GARDEN? I've searched the entire sanctuary and I haven't found it."

"Maybe you didn't know where to look," Colette said cryptically.

"Okay, I've had enough of your games," the mouse growled. "Stan, Max: GET THEM!"

At that moment, the Thea Sisters heard a

car horn! The sanctuary entrance was just a few feet away, and a red pickup truck came rumbling up.

A snout popped out from the passenger window, and they recognized it immediately.

"**Come on, friends!**" Aditi cried.

The four thugs were distracted by the unexpected interruption, and the Thea Sisters quickly took advantage. They darted toward the truck and quickly tossed their bicycles in the back before they **JUMPED** into the truck. Violet held the tapestry, and Nicky was the last to board, clutching the vial.

"Go, Dad, go!" Aditi said.

"What made you **come back** for us, Aditi?" Nicky asked as soon as it was clear they had gotten a safe head start.

"When I returned to the **restaurant**, my father told me that as soon as you had left,

THREE MICE had come by and asked about the five of you. He told them you were taking a trip to Lakh Bahosi, but I had a **bad feeling**. You didn't tell me much, but I knew you were searching for something precious, so I was worried. We waited a bit, but when you hadn't returned yet with the bikes, I convinced my dad to come and look for you."

"I've never been happier to see anymouse in my life!" Nicky sighed with relief as she leaned back against the seat and closed her eyes.

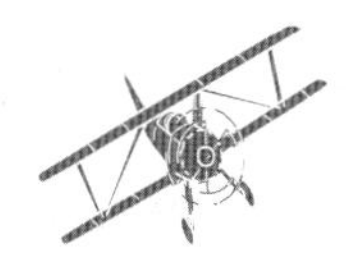

A DREAM FOR THE FUTURE

"I can't wait to get back to Mouseford Academy so I can put up my paws and relax for a bit!" Violet said as they waited for their bags at the Whale Island Airport.

"It really was an extraordinary trip," Paulina said.

"Trip?" Nicky said. "Don't you mean trips? We visited so many different places: Scotland, England, France, Mexico, and India. To think that we were just supposed to have a quiet vacation at a relaxing Scottish farm . . ."

"I know," Colette agreed. "I already miss Beitris. She was so happy that we were successful."

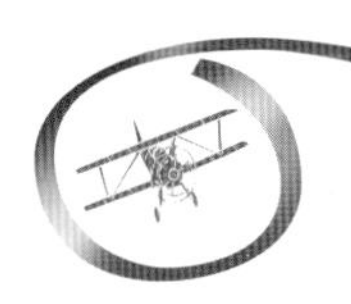

"There they are!" Pam exclaimed, **pointing** to the five backpacks slowly making their way down the conveyer belt.

Nicky quickly **GRABBED** her bag.

"I say we finish reading Aurora's journal tonight," Paulina proposed as they left the airport.

"Yes!" Colette agreed. "We've been **so busy**. I can't believe we haven't gotten through all the pages yet. But tonight we can have a **relaxing** evening rereading Aurora's words and continuing to relive the marvemouse adventure of the seven treasures."

And so, that evening, the five friends gathered together to read.

19th of April

Dear Diary,

It was so hard not to tell everything to my little sister, but I believe it's better this way. Now she has the key to find the alabaster garden, but the treasure is still safe.

The book spoke of six other places where there are treasures.

I am ready to go find the next one.

But once again I am convinced that the best solution would be to entrust it to one of my sisters.

I have a mission now, dear Diary: to find all the most precious treasures of the world and make sure that no one uses them for their own personal gain.

I will not stop until I have finished.

And when I have done it, I will return and retrieve each one. Then I'll make sure that they are preserved in the best way possible and can be enjoyed by all.

No one can stop my dream because our dreams make us who we are.

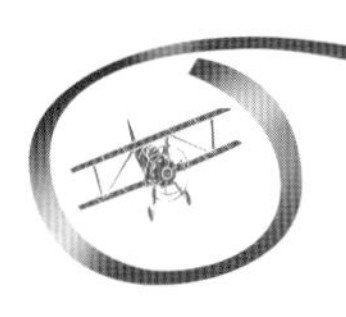

The Thea Sisters closed the **journal** and went to sleep. The exhaustion from their travels made it easy for everyone to fall asleep at once — everyone but Nicky, that is!

She lay awake in bed, thoughts ***racing*** through her head. The mysterious enemy who had been *CHASING* them from country to country had been uncovered. He was a descendent of **Jan von Klawitz**, and he shared Aurora's teacher's nasty intentions.

There were still six treasures out there, and something told Nicky he would not **STOP UNTIL HE FOUND THEM**. Perhaps she and her friends would soon find themselves in the middle of a new adventure to protect Aurora's dream.

AS ALWAYS, THE THEA SISTERS WOULD DO IT TOGETHER, LIKE TRUE SISTERS!

Don't miss any of these exciting Thea Sisters adventures!

Thea Stilton and the Dragon's Code

Thea Stilton and the Mountain of Fire

Thea Stilton and the Ghost of the Shipwreck

Thea Stilton and the Secret City

Thea Stilton and the Mystery in Paris

Thea Stilton and the Cherry Blossom Adventure

Thea Stilton and the Star Castaways

Thea Stilton: Big Trouble in the Big Apple

Thea Stilton and the Ice Treasure

Thea Stilton and the Secret of the Old Castle

Thea Stilton and the Blue Scarab Hunt

Thea Stilton and the Prince's Emerald

Thea Stilton and the Mystery on the Orient Express

Thea Stilton and the Dancing Shadows

Thea Stilton and the Legend of the Fire Flowers

Thea Stilton and the Spanish Dance Mission

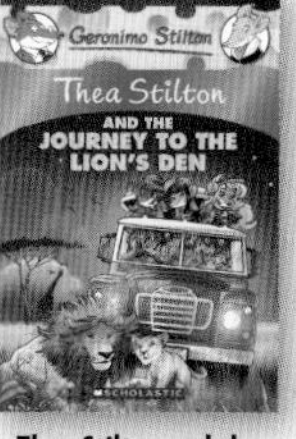

Thea Stilton and the Journey to the Lion's Den

Thea Stilton and the Great Tulip Heist

Thea Stilton and the Chocolate Sabotage

Thea Stilton and the Missing Myth

Thea Stilton and the Lost Letters

Thea Stilton and the Tropical Treasure

Thea Stilton and the Hollywood Hoax

Thea Stilton and the Madagascar Madness

Thea Stilton and the Frozen Fiasco

Thea Stilton and the Venice Masquerade

Thea Stilton and the Niagara Splash

Thea Stilton and the Riddle of the Ruins

Thea Stilton and the Phantom of the Orchestra

And check out my fabumouse special editions!

Thea Stilton: The Journey to Atlantis

Thea Stilton: The Secret of the Fairies

Thea Stilton: The Secret of the Snow

Thea Stilton: The Cloud Castle

Thea Stilton: The Treasure of the Sea

Thea Stilton: The Land of Flowers

Thea Stilton: The Secret of the Crystal Fairies